Western Front

Western Front

France: 1918 and 1944

Fred Mitchell

Order this book online at www.trafford.com
or email orders@trafford.com

Most Trafford titles are also available at major online book retailers.

Printed in the United States of America.

ISBN: 978-1-4269-5180-0 (sc)
ISBN: 978-1-4269-5190-9 (hc)
ISBN: 978-1-4269-5191-6 (e)

Library of Congress Control Number: 2010918497

Trafford rev. 01/12/2011

North America & International
toll-free: 1 888 232 4444 (USA & Canada)
phone: 250 383 6864 • fax: 812 355 4082

DEDICATION

To all soldiers who honorably and bravely faced each other in the course of the terrible times on the Western Front during both WWI and WWII.

Especially, to General Hasso Eccard von Manteuffel whose friendship and memory I cherish and so vividly remember.

Also, Shirley, dear Shirley.... Once more, my thanks. You are the wind beneath my sails.

BOOKS BY AUTHOR

WHEN RIVERS MEET
— *ISBN*: 0533-14958-4 (2005)

THE HINDENBURG'S FAREWELL
—*ISBN*: 1-4120-8901-8 (2006)

DECEMBER 7TH, 1941
—*ISBN*: 978-1-4251-4616-0 (2008)

BEYOND THE ARC
—*ISBN*: 978-1-4269-0312-0 (2010)

WESTERN FRONT (2011)

****

ABOUT THE AUTHOR

Mitchell has written several books regarding *historical time travel, which combines history with fiction.* He has taken another trip. If you liked his other stories, you'll like this one too. It's kinda different.

Mitchell was Vice President of the prestigious Civil War Round Table of Chicago during the centennial years 1961-1965, is retired from the "Old" Bell Telephone System, and currently resides in Mesa, Arizona with his wife, Shirley.

CONTENTS

PART 1

SORTIE

FRANCE - WESTERN FRONT, 1918

My name is First Lieutenant Mathew Dale Mitchell, age 23, of the United States Air Corps. I was born in 1895 in Springfield, Illinois and throughout my early years I became more and more impressed by the new marvels of my time, flying machines called airplanes.

In 1910 when I was fifteen I saw my first airplane. It had just arrived by truck at the Springfield flying field which was nothing more than a large mowed area. There was one building which served as both a machine shop and hanger.

I sorta chuckled, the airplane looked to me like a large kite. There was a small motor at the front, a seat for the pilot, two fabric covered wings, and at the tail end a strange looking apparatus they called a rudder. To top it off the plane was mounted on what looked very much like a pair of undersized bicycle wheels.

I was excited at meeting the pilot, James Watt, and a couple hours later watched as he took her up. At first the little plane sputtered and wheezed before the motor finally smoothed out. The crew next pushed Watt onto a smoothly cut row of grass they called a runway. The little plane wheezed again, sounded a couple of loud bangs, and began to slowly roll down the runway. It gained speed, and *oh, good lord*, it rose slowly into the air reaching an unthinkable altitude of about 300 feet at an amazing speed of maybe 30 mph. Pilot Watt flew his craft around the airfield twice, switched off the motor, and glided to a landing.

As the plane rolled to a stop everyone ran to it and pushed and pulled it back to the hanger area. Watt, his face now splattered with oil, was all smiles. *I was hooked*; the result was I spent most of my spare time at the airport fiddling with everything I could get my hands on. My devoted efforts so impressed the owners of the airfield that in 1912 they hired me full time to help service their fleet of planes which had grown to three.

My love for flying continued unabated. In 1915 with the aid of a close friend of our family, U.S. Senator George McClellan of Illinois, I enlisted in the fledgling United States Air Corps and received an assignment as a flying cadet. I graduated in 1916 having soloed in a Flying Jenny, at this time America's only war plane. It was a solid craft but carried no weaponry. At last I had earned my wings and with them a promotion to Second Lieutenant.

By 1916 pilots in Europe are beginning to arm themselves and air warfare is losing its chivalrousness. Pilots now are throwing themselves into deadly jousts similar to the knights of yore, except they are now being fought at

10,000 feet altitude, traveling in excess of 100 mph and armed with far more deadly weapons than a lance.

In the summer of 1917 our training squadron received six new Sopwith Camel fighter planes from England and I was selected among a group of ten pilots to learn to fly them. We were taught aerobatics and fighter tactics by officers from the Royal Flying Corps. Graduating at the top of my class I was promoted to First Lieutenant. Though as yet I had no combat experience, in my mind it would only be a matter of time before it would come.

Today, March 15, 1918 my crusade began. I am preparing to leave Springfield by train for New York. On the 21st my contingent shall board a troop ship for France. It is with great sadness that I am leaving as my darling wife, Connie, is with child and due within a month. My last few days at home have been a combination of sadness, mixed with pleasure, and of course anticipation. It seemed my head was in a daze with so much on my mind.

Connie worries constantly about me and I reassure her that everything will be OK. "This is a job that needs to be done for America, for you, for our child, and hopefully for the world to be forever again without war."

The last week has so quickly evaporated into the past. Connie, mom and dad, along with several friends loaded into several cars and we chugged along the brick streets to downtown Springfield.

I felt resplendent in my army uniform and said my good- byes, kissed Connie passionately, patted her belly saying, "See ya someday my child." I saluted, boarded the train, waved, threw a last kiss, and looked about at the Springfield skyline, not knowing when or if I should ever see it again.

The trip to New York was astounding as I watched the country pass. For the first time in my life I realized how huge the United States was, soon to find out my education had only begun.

Next came New York City, huge, sprawling, and way beyond anything I had ever imagined. As we arrived in New York, we were quickly herded onto our buses and driven to our port of embarkation where we boarded a troopship crammed full of every imaginable sort. My quarters in the officers' section was small and shared with three others, none of which were from the Air Corps.

A monumental revelation came as I watched the Atlantic ocean pass beneath our keel. Being from the Midwest I was truly a landlubber. The only sailing I had ever experienced was in a rowboat on Lake Springfield. It seemed like the world was truly passing me by. I mused, *We may as well be on our way to another planet.*

Our troop ship was a converted passenger ship circa 1895. The food was adequate, but most didn't give a damn as seasickness made the crossing miserable for everyone. Days crawled by before our ship arrived at our port of disembarkation, Le Havre, France. As land first appeared off the starboard side, I thought, *France, your saviors have finally arrived.* Everyone was more than anxious to get off the ship, and sincerely hoped someday we would enjoy a home cooked meal again.

Finally, we were introduced to the beautiful French countryside. A bumpy, noisy, crammed two day train ride where everything seemed so quiet and peaceful, we were inclined to wonder where the war was. However, we would soon find our answers. Our clickety-click, bumpy train ride over rough tracks was accompanied by a half day bus ride over some really bad roads, more like wide undeveloped paths; the homes and countryside began to offer shocking statements as to the omnipresence of the war. Finally somewhat disheveled, tired, and hungry, along with a few other soldiers of all ranks, I was delivered to my new home, Cerlot Aerodrome at Cerlot, France.

* * * * *

Suddenly Squadron Leader, First Lieutenant Mathew Dale Mitchell of the United States Army Air Corps, on 3 April, 1918 was introduced to his first combat posting. I was met by an orderly who took my bags and led me to my quarters which were Spartan but the bed looked comfortable. As Squadron Leader I had a private room which until a few days ago had been occupied by First Lieutenant Howard Tuft. From my orderly I understood he had been shot down and duly reported missing.

After quickly unpacking my bags, I grabbed my orders and hurried to the commanding officer's office. There I was greeted by Major Robert Taylor who stood, six feet tall, with wavy black hair, mustache, and with pipe in hand he reflected a rather debonair appearance. He returned my salute saying, "Lieutenant Mitchell, how good it is you are here. Your Number 26 Squadron is fortunately standing down for a couple of days so this will provide me with an opportunity to introduce you to your new command."

Quickly Major Taylor added, "You see, Mitchell, of late the Germans have been quite active in this vicinity; thus, you will find your squadron doing all sorts of nasty little things from flying morning patrols to strafing enemy airfields, trenches, and everything in between. Glad to have you, ole boy, your record looks impeccable but I'm sure you'll find combat somewhat a different bag.

"I asked your second in command, wingman 2nd Lieutenant Charles W. London, to drop by. We call him CW; here he comes now." CW was six feet tall, 190 pounds, a ruddy complexion, moustache, brown hair, and a memorable smile. After introductions, I added, "CW, please call me Mat." I also noticed most everyone sported a mustache and considered it might be a good idea if I had one too.

The three of us spent the next couple hours pouring over charts and maps of my squadron's patrol area. I learned my five remaining pilots had a cumulative total of twelve verified kills while experiencing a loss of only two aircraft. Additionally Lieutenant Tuft who was listed as missing had destroyed four more. I was acutely aware that my grand total of zero kills didn't help the squadron's status, but felt confident I would soon correct my standing. I thanked Major Taylor and asked CW to introduce me to the boys. We walked into the adjacent ready room where the other four members of my squadron were playing pinochle. They arose in unison, saluted, and stood rigidly at attention. My first command to them was, "At ease, gentlemen."

CW began, "Sir, here is the finest squadron in France, bar none. Let me introduce you to:

2nd Lt. John Henry Dowd, from Salem, Il, 2 kills
2nd Lt. Carl Abbott from, Sikeston, MO, 1 kill
2nd Lt. Billy(the kid) Kane, from Billings, MT, 3 kills
2nd Lt. Frank Purvis, from Dallas, TX, 2 kills."

I said, "Thank you, Lieutenant, and I conclude you have the remaining four kills. I am impressed and tell you I shall endeavor to catch up." CW added, "I am sure you will, Sir. Now come on down to the flight line and meet the most important men in the squadron, our chief mechanic Staff Sergeant Francois *Frenchy* Dubois, and his crew."

As we approached the flight line I saw the six planes, all British Sopwith Camels, of Number 26 Squadron glistening in the late afternoon sun. Sergeant Dubois spotted us, snapped stiffly to attention, appropriately presented me with a rather oily, but dutifully respectable salute.

Over the next couple days I continued my orientation with Major Taylor regarding squadron protocol. Additionally my squadron flew several "get acquainted missions" over friendly territory. My first war patrol was 6 April with revelry at 0330 and takeoff at 0515.

It was a reconnaissance mission over German lines to check supply build-up, which often forecasted offense movements.

Our sortie wasn't too exciting, but it was enough for my first combat mission and that was important. Our patrol lasted two hours, seemed longer; however, I was pleased with my squadron's formations, interpretations of hand signals, and coordination.

After landing we were debriefed by Major Taylor in our squad room. He seemed pleased with my report, and said, "See you all this evening for drinks at the officers' club." To which he received a hearty, "Here! Here!"

When I returned to my room, there was a letter on my bed from Connie. I quickly opened it and read every line over and over. Connie said she was doing fine, missed me, but assured me she was feeling good and was under great care, so not to worry. I was greatly relieved.

Number 26 Squadron's next sortie was scheduled for 11 April with takeoff at 0630. This morning it would be a deep penetration behind German lines, raiding a designated aerodrome and any other targets of opportunity which might present themselves. After noting our orders, I thought *finally combat*! My heart rate accelerated a bit, but soon the excitement turned to one of anticipation; however, I was confident I would do well and let any feeling of anxiousness go for what it was, an emotion and only that.

During the ensuing days we continued to review our protocols and talked about possibilities such as going down behind enemy lines and so forth. To the rest of the squadron this was old hat, but for me, their fearless leader, it was a *number one concern.*

* * * * *

11 April arrived and I was excited, my first hard core taste of combat. Any previous fears were now buried somewhere deep within my psyche. As our gallant

group walked to the flight line we could hear our planes being warmed up under the watchful eyes of Chief Mechanic Sergeant Dubois. Our Sopwith Camels were magnificent flying machines and the squadron was very proud of them. I harkened back to that day in 1910 when I saw my first airplane; what a change eight years have made! It was now 0545 and still dark as I walked up and down the line with Sergeant Dubois. The twinkling stars heralded a clear day for our forage into enemy territory, a good day for noticing enemy movements.

While the pilots were still going over their pre-flight preparations, I hurried back to Major Robert (Rob) Taylor's headquarters for any last minute questions or orders. Taylor was a well thought of commanding officer who in ten months of active service before accepting this position had destroyed 22 enemy planes and received the Silver Flying Cross with Valor.

I had no kills but hoped someday to do as well as Taylor. Major Taylor greeted me, "Good morning, Lieutenant. Is number 26 Squadron ready to go?" I saluted, "Sir, we are good to go. Do you have any last minute instructions, Sir?" Taylor returned my salute, "No, Lieutenant, there are no new instructions. Just get out there, get every detail you can, and remember no fighting unless you are attacked."

I responded, "Yes, Sir, I have already provided my pilots with those instructions." Taylor saluted, said, "OK, Mitchell, bring us back some good stuff." I saluted, replied, "I'll try, Sir," did an about face, and hurriedly rushed to the flight line. Our six little planes stood lined up with all my pilots ready in their cockpits.

On the way I took a moment to check on my readiness. My thick leather flying boots were tightly laced, my heavy leather flight coat was snugged up around my neck, and the heavy oaken fire wall which separated me from the engine was in place. These were my best defenses against an engine fire. Parachutes were supposed to be a pilots last chance at surviving a fire, however they were not very dependable. At 0625 I arrived at my plane, stepped onto the lower wing, slung my right leg over the cockpit wall, and snuggled down into the seat with the stick between my knees. I adjusted my goggles as Francois patted me on my leather helmet. I raised my right arm signaling it was time for takeoff. The other pilots raised theirs. They were ready.

As I dropped my arm the ground crews kicked away our wheel chucks and in groups of twos we sputtered, roared, and bounced down the grassy runway. Suddenly our Sopwith Camel's noses pointed skyward and soon we were airborne cruising along at 3800 feet.

We leveled off, and per our plans, we paired off with one plane mapping and noting any appropriate movements, while the second plane defended against enemy intrusions. I would do the mapping, while Second Lieutenant Charles W. London (CW), my wingman, would defend against any enemy attack. I felt comfortable with CW who already had drawn blood with four kills to his credit.

Our small contingent flew on until shortly we crossed no-man's-land into German air space. The sun had arisen bright; a clear day lay ahead for our low level recon flight. With our binoculars we could see good detail as far as the horizon.

To my right leg mounted on a clipboard was strapped a map of the area. While my attention was directed toward the ground, CW was watching my rear and above me, especially into the sun, a favorite attack direction on a day like this. After ten minutes of mapping and dodging sporadic fire from the ground, which was generally not too effective, suddenly I saw the flash of a flare to the front and slightly above me and knew it was CW notifying me of a German attack from above.

I saw the other two sections of my squadron doing the same thing and suddenly we were in a dogfight outnumbered 2 to 1 by one of Germany's finest fighter aircraft, the Fokker D-7 tri-plane. Moments later in the distance I saw a plane explode in a brilliant ball of fire and begin its earthly plummet to immortality. At my distance it was impossible to tell, German or American; I just hoped for the best.

I knew there was a Fokker on my tail and began to sway my Sopwith Camel right to left, closed my throttle, and sharply dove straight down. Fooled at first by my antics the German raced by me at full throttle. Noting that CW had also inherited a pursuer, I opened full throttle, pulled my stick into my ribcage and my Sopwith Camel raced upward directly at CW's pursuer. Closing fast on the German, I cut loose with my two forward firing 30 caliber machine guns. My aim was good, the pilot slumped forward, and smoke began pouring from the engine as his plane began a death spiral toward earth. It was not my favorite sight, and my heart was pounding. It was my first kill, to be confirmed by CW, who thankfully clasped his fists above his head.

* * * * *

However, euphoria was short lived for strangely *my stick would not move forward,* my plane continued to climb, and at 8,000 feet I passed into a bank of dense white, fluffy clouds. The French countryside and all else had totally vanished; for several minutes I was alone and beginning to find it difficult to breathe due to a lack of oxygen.

Finally my stick began to respond ever so slightly to my adjustments, and as I slowly pushed it forward the plane began a gradual descent to 6,500 feet where I escaped below the confines of the mysterious cloud bank. I could now breathe better and my plane seemed again to be functioning properly.

Now only small white cloud banks obstructed my view. I reduced my air speed to 90 mph, raised my goggles and looked at the country below me. It did not look the same! *What the duce has happened? Where am I? This can't be France.* I took my binoculars and focused them trying to locate something recognizable.

The world below was filled with green pastures and wide roadways where vehicles of all sizes and shapes rushed headlong at each other. There were several small villages within my view, and as I continued flying my amazement was not abated. The structures were definitely not of French, or even German design. Even the churches appeared different.

Suddenly to my front in the distance something familiar caught my attention.... Giant runways sprawled across a huge, beyond anything I could imagine, what appeared to be an aerodrome.

Then as if to further my confusion, a large dark colored sphere-like flying object with a white star on it's wing and fuselage swished past me and my little plane shuddered so badly I feared it's wings might fall off. The roar was almost untenable and the flying object rapidly began to recede into the distance, disappearing behind a cloud formation.

I think there was a pilot aboard; there was no way to estimate the object's speed, but compared to my 95 mph, it was as if my Sopwith Camel was standing still.

As the sphere moved away, something dropped down from it's underside. I concluded it must be the landing gear in preparation for landing at that aerodrome ahead. I continued to cut my ignition switch off, then on, in order to fly lower and lower hoping to eventually land. *Good, God, where is this place?*

At this time the officer in charge of operations at the aerodrome, Major Paul Dawson, was advised by the officer in charge of monitoring incoming flights that he had something unusual on his approach radar screen.

A small unidentified object flying at 800 feet, lowering its altitude at a rate of 100 feet per minute, closing at a speed of 92 mph, and on a heading to land on runway five. At the same time, the pilot of the interceptor which had just landed reported he had over flown what appeared to be a World War I biplane bearing old United States Air Corps markings, the white star with the red ball center in a blue background. He concluded his report with, "Must be some nut from a flying circus."

Observations all indicated the unidentified plane would soon land on runway number five. The officer in charge immediately aborted all outgoing traffic, rerouted all incoming traffic, and directed emergency vehicles into position at runway five. Major Dawson quickly grabbed two security sergeants and said, "Come, let's get the hell over to runway five, we got some nut trying to land an old bi-plane there." They raced off in their staff car and sped away.

Lieutenant Mitchell was now two miles from touchdown flying at 300 feet. Though still confused he continued to cut power to his engine, turning it off and then on again, the only way to land his plane. It caused a *bluurp, bluurp, bluurp* sound as the engine cut in and out allowing his plane to reduce speed and settle into its landing.

In my cockpit I was overwhelmed at the sight advancing before me. Huge airplanes lined my approach route, their wingspans seemed large enough to land my plane on, and red trucks loaded with men wearing what looked like white bags, were rushing toward me. Also there was that plane which only moments ago swooshed by. I wondered where the pilot was?

Back in Cerlot, it was 0830 and four planes, what remained of my squadron, were returning from their mission. Major Rob Taylor and Chief Mechanic Dubois were anxiously waiting for them to land. The air was filled with the familiar *bluurp, bluurp, bluurp* of their arrival. A gentle wisp of smoke trailed behind the last plane.

Upon landing 2nd Lieutenant Charles, CW, Wilson's plane coasted to a stop. He pulled himself from his cockpit and was met by Major Taylor. "Sir, on behalf of Squadron leader Mitchell, I wish to report the loss of Second Lieutenant Davidson's plane. It was hit by ground fire, exploded in air and plummeted to the ground, Sir. I am sorry to report he could never have survived. Second Lieutenant Davidson was a student pilot only yesterday assigned to the 26th for combat introduction. *How unfair this war is…He never got a round off and it's over.*

"As for Squadron Leader Mitchell, he shot down a Heine who was on my tail, then his ship disappeared into a cloud bank and has not been seen since." Taylor considered that Mitchell would undoubtedly show up; however, as time passed and he didn't, the best Taylor could hope for was Mitchell was down in German territory and now a prisoner. Taylor accepted CW's report and told him to report to debriefing.

* * * * *

Meanwhile back at wherever this is, I taxied up to a giant plane which had no props, only two gigantic large round scoops, one on each wing? Never had I seen, or even thought of, anything like it. As I sat stupefied, Major Dawson and his escorts arrived. They leaped from their automobile before it had even stopped, rushed to the side of my plane, and the two sergeants pointed their pistols at my head. They definitely had my attention.

Dawson hollered, "Who the hell are you, and what are you doing here?" For a few moments I sat frozen like a chunk of ice before saluting and replying, "Sir, I am Squadron Leader First Lieutenant Mathew D. Mitchell, Aero Pursuit Squadron 26 from Cerlot, France. And who, Sir, who the hell are you? I don't know what I am doing here, wherever this damn place is, Sir?"

The major slowly and awkwardly returned my salute, answering, "You, Lieutenant, are at the United States Air Force base at Pawtucket, Delaware. I am Major Paul Dawson, Operations Officer." I stuttered a response, "Err, Sir, you must be jesting me." Dawson restated his response, "You are in one heap of trouble. Landing an unauthorized plane at a military airfield without any clearance or authorization is not taken lightly."

I responded, "Pardon me, Major, but a few minutes ago I was in aerial combat over German lines fighting off Fokkers with others of my squadron. And, Sir, I don't have any idea on how the hell I got here, wherever you say this place might be. And beggin' you're pardon, Sir, but one of us is leaking oil from his crankcase. One minute I'm spittin' lead at the Germans, the next minute I'm landing here. You figure out what the shit is goin' on here, Sir, and then let me know. Please ask your boys to put their pistols down, I ain't goin' nowhere." Major Dawson agreed, ordering his sergeants to put away their pistols. I was somewhat relieved.

Major Dawson asked me to cut my engine and to follow him. I complied, asking him to please see to it that my plane was well cared for as I would be needing it later. He smiled politely; *I thought, hopefully, that was good news.* He said, "Don't worry, Lieutenant, I will see to it." I climbed from my Sopwith Camel, got in his staff car, *boy what a beauty, never saw anything like her!* We sped off to his office and passed an amazing array of airplanes of all sizes and shapes. What really struck me was there wasn't a propeller in sight. *How do these thing fly?*

When we arrived at Major Dawson's office he asked me to have a seat. As I looked around, there was no doubt, I wasn't in 1918 France. There were items of furniture and stuff which were foreign to me. As I sat in amazement, Dawson commanded his aide to, "Get Captains Alton, Baylor, and Carson here on the double." I smirked quietly to myself and concluded, *they must be the ABC boys.*

While we waited for their arrival, I asked Major Dawson if it would be alright for me to take a peek around the office as it was crammed with lots of strange appearing machinery? He replied, "Of course, Lieutenant, come on and I'll show you around." As we did, he pointed out something he called radar, explaining the little blips and figures which displayed on their screens the location of any flying objects within a hundred miles, calculating and displaying their speed, size, and distance from the airport. He concluded with, "We watched your progress as you landed, Lieutenant."

On another screen I saw what he described as GPS (Global Positioning System). With this, he explained, the location of most any moving thing on earth, plane, ship, or even a moving vehicle, can be pinpointed. Then I listened for awhile to what was evidently talk between pilots and people they called controllers. Didn't understand much they were saying, but it must beat the hell out of communicating by waving your arms and shooting off flares.

By this time the ABC boys had arrived and my brain was already spinning, *this damn stuff is scary.* We returned to Major Dawson's office and he introduced me to apparently his goon squad, Doctor Alton, Medical Officer, Captain Baylor, Chaplin, and Doctor Carlson, Psychologist. I saluted each in turn, took my seat, and awaited the worst.

Major Dawson related my tale, as he referred to notes from my statement, and asked them to decipher what it meant. He added his initial investigation supported what I had told him, but of course it didn't make sense. "His plane was checked out as vintage, down to the ammo in the guns, the oil in the crankcase, as well as his clothing. Here is his identification card, and as you can see it appears authentic: *Squadron Leader, 1st Lieutenant Mathew D. Mitchell, United States Air Corps, Aero Pursuit Squadron No. 26, Cerlot, France, born November 13, 1895, Illinois, USA.... Issue Date: March 23, 1918....Protestant.*"

From the beginning the ABC boys seemed friendly and sincerely interested in me. Dr. Carlson, the psychiatrist, appeared to be in charge. He began by handing me a page full of questions and said, "Lieutenant, please answer these in the order they appear." I looked at the paper he handed me and felt kinda like a guinea pig. How old are you? Where were you born? What are your parent's names? Where do they reside? Are you married? If so, what is your wife's full name, including maiden name and age? Any children? If so, what is/are their full name/names and ages? What schools did you attend? Where did you attend flying school? Where and when did you join the army? Who was your commanding officer?

Finally, I told them, "Will do my best to accommodate you, but enough is enough. In fact I will do your list right now." Which I did and handed it to Dr. Carlson:

Self: Mathew Dale Mitchell, b.1895, Springfield, Illinois (W) Connie (Aarlsen) b. 1896, Jacksonville, Illinois

Parents: Frederick H., b. 1870 & Thelma (Barrett) Mitchell, b. 1871, Residence: Springfield, Illinois

Schools attended: PS3, 1909, Springfield HS, 1913

Flying School: Capitol Air, Springfield, IL, certified 1915 enlisted US Army Air Corps, 1915....1917, arrived Cerlot Aerodrome, France 4-3-1918

Commanding Officer: Cerlot France, Major Robert Taylor (I added parenthetically, *he is, not was, my commanding officer.)*

"Here, Sir, and now I am just out of gas. Can I just go to my plane and leave this incredible place? Dr. Carlson politely but emphatically said, "Lieutenant, no you can not leave, at least not yet. Are you hungry?" I jumped on that, "Yes, Sir, famished and thirsty for a beer, too. This has already been a difficult and long day." Dr. Carlson smiled, the first human reaction from him so far. As the ABC boys left, Chaplin Baylor told me he would return after I had eaten.

At last… my meal arrived along with a large stein of frothy beer. A great assortment of cold cuts, cheeses, fruits, and a large piece of apple pie. Light fare, but attractively laid out, and I dove right in. The beer really topped it off. As I finished Chaplin Baylor returned and said, "Lieutenant, it is my duty to advise you that tonight and until further notice you are the guest of the United States Air Force. I'll accompany you to your billet and stay with you for awhile to see if you have any questions regarding your stay here." I thanked him and told him I would appreciate just being alone, but perhaps a little later another beer would really help. Chaplin Baylor grinned, said, "OK, Mat, come with me and I'll take you to your quarters."

At 0800 the next morning I was called to Major Dawson's office and in attendance were Colonels Myers and Davis. It appeared my importance may have received a promotion. They asked me to take a seat at the large oak conference table where I felt like the only person on this planet. In this place in the year 2000, so they tell me, there were no friends from my old squadron, in fact no one I even knew, no nothing; I felt like a stranger without a home.

Major Dawson began, "Lieutenant Mitchell, our people have been working hard to substantiate the information you provided us and we are somewhat stymied. Everything you told us has been confirmed!" I replied, "If you, Sir, are confused, what do you think that makes me?" My mind was blank, *Of course, I am for real, it's these guys who must be imposters. This can not be the year 2000.* I leaned back in my chair, took a large sip from my water glass, put my arms behind my head, lightly laughed, and said, "Alright, Sirs, where the deuce do we go from here?"

Dawson said, "Mat, I do have some good news. You are the father of a baby boy named Frederick Dale." I was not surprised, been expecting it. But a boy, now that was great news. He was named after my grandfather Mitchell and that made me happy.

For Major Dawson, Colonels Myers and Davis, this left them with one very large dilemma. They had here an officer who in 1918 was declared missing while flying a mission over German lines, and then later reported missing and presumed dead to a wife with a son just born. Now he is here, alive, well, and probably has living descendants via his son, Frederick Dale.

* * * * *

I quickly stood and replied, “Sirs, here’s my idea. Gas up my plane and let me try to take her home. Perhaps if I fly into a cloud formation similar to the one from whence I came, it will reverse whatever it was that brought me here. Sounds fantastic but what the heck! To me, trying anything is better than remaining here in a place where I don’t belong nor want to be. My wife, my new son, my friends, and *my war*, they are not here! So, damn it, Sirs, please, please, turn me loose and let me try to get home.” The room remained very still.

I sat down, crossed my fingers, and waited. Colonel Myers, Executive Officer of the base, spoke first. “Lieutenant, considering your situation you have reason to feel the way you do and we respect that. However, we can not at this time make any definitive decisions. There is far more to investigate and to consider before arriving at any course of action. Please understand.”

After a time I again stood, wiped my brow, and answered, "Sir, as much as I wish to go home you are undoubtedly right but, Sir, please don't forget my request, and make your decision soon." He replied, "Lieutenant Mitchell, you have my assurance, we will not forget your request."

Major Dawson added, "We will reconvene here the day after tomorrow at 0900. In the meantime, Lieutenant, I am assigning Staff Sergeant William (Bill) Karr of my staff to be your aide and guide while you are our guest." I saluted saying, "Thank you, Sir."

Staff Sergeant William Karr entered, saluted, and was introduced to me. He was about my size and age, six feet, brown crew cut, blue eyes, and a great grin. He shook my hand, told me he was very pleased to be my aide for the duration of my stay, and said we would go to the officers' club for awhile and sorta line up my activities for the next couple of days. I exclaimed, "Fine, Sergeant, let's do it."

At the officers' club we were ushered to a booth in the VIP section, thanks to Major Dawson, where we would be quite alone. Sergeant Karr ordered us two steins of German Pilsner Beer and for a moment I forgot where and when this was. We might be at war with the Germans, but never with their beer. I said, "Good choice, Bill."

Staff Sergeant Karr laid out plans for the rest of today and tomorrow: "This afternoon we will go for a walk through the base, visit a couple of hangers which include antique aircraft from your WWI and also from WWII which took place during the years 1939-1945 between many of the same antagonists. Except this time Italy and Japan were allied with Germany. Yep, Lieutenant, we had to do it all over again. Your war ended on November 11, 1918 at 11 minutes past 1100 hours.

"This evening, Sir, we will attend a dance at the officers' club, and I will obtain a uniform for you, today's vintage, of course. How does this sound, Sir?" Of course I was flabbergasted and told Bill so. "This is still beyond belief, but I have never felt this was only a dream. That's what makes this whole damn thing so incredible. And by the way, Bill, from now on unless otherwise dictated, it's Mat." He replied, "Fine with me, Sir." We both had a good laugh.

After a light lunch we left and shortly entered a huge hanger. The first thing which caught my eye was a Flying Jenny, a Fokker D-7, and a Sopwith Camel like mine. It was like a homecoming. Then we visited the WWII exhibit which included planes that Bill identified as an American B-17 Flying Fortress, a P-40 and P-47 American fighters. Next was an English Spitfire, a Japanese Zero, and a German Messerschmitt (Me109). I marveled at the technical advances in aviation made during the ensuing 25 years. Bill added, "Mat, you ain't seen anything yet."

As we left the hanger, Bill said, "Tomorrow afternoon, Mat, you will have an opportunity to fly piggyback aboard one of our modern jet fighters, and I am sure Captain Morris, your pilot, will let you handle the stick." I thought, *Good God, am I ever looking forward to that.* Bill continued, "After that we will visit command center where all flight activities for the base are administered." Finally as we pulled up to my quarters he added, "Mat, I will pick you up tonight at 1900. Your new uniform is hanging in your closet." I replied, "My thanks, Bill," returned his salute and went inside. *Wow, what a day. Sure wish Major Taylor and CW could be here. Wouldn't that be the hoots!*

Staff Sergeant Karr arrived at 1900 in a staff car, pretty heady stuff for a lieutenant, but I figured, *what the hell, guess things like this don't happen every day*. Bill saluted, opened the door, and I sat down in the front seat with him for our short drive to the officers' world of frivolity, the officers' club.

When we arrived Bill introduced me to the headwaiter, Manuel, and then left. I was ushered by Manuel to a table near the rear of the dining room where two lieutenants and a captain with their dates were seated, and introduced to a young lady who I supposed would be my date for the evening. Her name was Sandy Greer, a secretary in the command center, cute, blonde, blue-eyed, great smile, and about 5'7". I was not at all displeased.

Introductions followed. Captain Benjamin Morris would be the pilot for my flight tomorrow, and Lieutenants Clifford Hawes and Daniel Molders would act as our wingmen. He then introduced their dates: Joyce Manners, Carol Brown, and his date, Pat Barnes. Captain Morris continued, "OK, gentlemen, now that formalities are over, for the balance of this evening we are, Ben and Carol, Cliff and Joyce, Dan and Carol, Sandy and Mat. Let's order drinks and I will propose a toast to our visiting dignitary." He raised his arm and a waiter appeared post haste. Everyone ordered a martini, or a glass of wine. It was good they took my order last as I would have ordered a beer. Quickly I adjusted my sights and asked for a glass of French Chablis.

When the drinks arrived, Ben stood, raised his glass and said, "Ladies and Gentlemen, I propose a toast to our distinguished guest. *We are honored to have a visitor such as you, Lieutenant Mitchell. Not just a person from another time, but one from a war long past. Hereto your time has only existed with us via photographs and history books. But you, Sir, are here, with us tonight, and 82 years away from your friends and your war. We salute you, Mathew Mitchell, wish your stay here to be enjoyable and fruitful, and wherever or whenever you leave us, remember that our spirits will forever ride beside you."* Everyone raised their glasses and in a single voice responded, "*Here, here*!"

I was considerably shaken and had to recover my senses before replying…. Finally, I spoke, "*Sandy, Ben, Pat, Cliff, Joyce, Dan, and Carol, thank you so very much. I badly need friends right now, and I accept your offer to ride with me wherever that might be, right now or whenever.*

"I feel so small coming here when fighting a war in the air in 1918 must seem so archaic to you. But when you are up there, without radios, parachutes, and radar, I tell you it is scary, thrilling, and gives you a blast which is unexplainable. But let me just say, as a little black sheep that has definitely lost his way, I couldn't have found a better pasture. Thank you, my friends. I shall cherish you forever." I sat down and everyone clapped and cheered. For a moment the dining room quieted wondering what was going on, but quickly the band started up and things returned to normal. I was very grateful. The toast really made me feel a part of this group.

The rest of the evening went fine. We danced, didn't recognize any tunes, except for the waltzes which I didn't do very well. Sandy did her best, we laughed a lot, she tried hard, and I answered a lot of questions about 1918.

At 2330 we enjoyed a last dance, then Bill arrived and took us to our quarters. On the way I told Sandy how much I enjoyed our evening and thanked her for putting up with me. While walking to her door I said, "Sandy, I do not know what happens next to me, but if I am here for awhile, could I call on you again?" She smiled, put her arm on my shoulder, looked into my eyes, said, "Of course, Lieutenant Mitchell, it would be my pleasure, call me," and she gave me her card. Unsure of myself, I replied, "Thank you, Sandy, for a wonderful evening, goodnight." I wanted so very much to hug and kiss her as an expression of my appreciation, but not wanting to be misunderstood, didn't. I just shook her hand.

The next morning Bill joined me and after a light breakfast we walked to hanger number 3 which housed two giant cargo planes which were similar to the ones I noticed while landing here. Bill told me they were some of the largest planes in the world. As we watched the loading crew was prepping one with supplies for a flight from Delaware to Hawaii, nonstop all the way across the United States and the Pacific Ocean. I found this almost unbelievable, and the plane was so huge I imagined *flying my Sopwith Camel right inside it and landing.* The crew drove three, what Bill called Humvees, up the rear ramp into the plane, parked them, and secured the vehicles with chain-like ropes. Next huge containers were loaded one after another. In one load this massive airplane could provide provisions for a whole company of men for a month. I shook my head jokingly, *could put my whole squadron in here, planes and all.*

From there we boarded a similar plane, normally crewed by a crew of 8: pilot, co-pilot, navigator, cargo-master, chief-engineer, and three handlers. I was informed these giants could if necessary be refueled while in flight by an airborne fuel tanker. *An airborne what?* It blew my mind. Onboard we visited various *crew* stations. *My God, the pilot cockpits were almost the size of my plane* and I just shook my head at the maze of gauges, dials, and handles. I thought, *how could anyone ever understand so many things and fly at the same time?*

On my plane all I had was a stick, an engine on-off switch, altimeter, oil and fuel gauges which sometimes worked, and an air speed indicator. There was no radio, only hand signals and an occasional flare were all that were available for communication between plane and ground. My landing approach system consisted of a windsock at the airfield and more often than not, a little luck.

After lunch came the occasion I had been waiting for, *my flight in a modern jet fighter plane.* I was shown mock-ups of a jet engine, and told how it worked. My God, it's like a giant Roman Candle that kids fire off on the 4th of July, and *I'm gonna fly in one of them*.... I laughed. *You bet your biffy I am. If I can fly a Sopwith Camel, I can handle one of these babies.*

After a visit to our plane we went to the pilot's ready room where they outfitted me with a flying suit, leather coat, boots, and helmet. I looked and felt like a man from outer space. Captain Ben Morris and Lieutenants Cliff Hawes and Dan Molders, our wingmen, were attired in their finery, and they chuckled as they watched my reactions. Ben said, "Mat, you'll be pleased to have these things on when we takeoff." I retorted, "Yup, imagine they might come in handy, but what are all these plugs for?" Ben answered, "Oh, don't worry about those, your ground attendants will see to it that you are properly plugged in." I thought, *Good Lord, this poor little sheep is certainly in a strange pasture.*

Finally, we walked outside where a special vehicle waited to transport us to our planes which were sitting side-by-side on the tarmac, their canopies open, and although I could hear no sound, their engines were idling. Interceptors I think they called them. *They looked like bombers to me; I was both anxious and exhilarated.*

Off in the distance, across the flight line, I caught a glimpse of my Sopwith Camel sitting outside a hanger as if she was an interested spectator to all that was happening around her. Thus, before entering the rear compartment of the cockpit of my "rocket ship," I turned to her, threw a salute her way, then climbed inside. Handlers suddenly appeared on both sides of me, helped me quickly to sit down, secured my harnesses, and attached all my cords to the various plugs. I felt more than weird.

With a loud crunch ... *our canopy slammed shut.* I looked around and could see our wingmen's planes suddenly accelerate. Then our plane began a slow roll. Captain Ben Morris's calm voice jarred me as he said to me via my headphone, "Mat, soon we will be airborne and I will make a steep climb to 20,000 feet. So hang on and enjoy the view." *20,000 feet, holy shit, what does he mean hang on?*

Before I could ask, Ben pushed his throttle to full open and we raced down the runway so fast buildings and everything else blurred into a vast nothingness. Interesting that it was quite still, only a distinct swishing sound. Abruptly we lifted off, almost straight up, and all I could see was the back of Ben's helmet and sky for it seemed like only seconds, until we leveled off.

I looked out and down. *Wow!* I could see the world below me and it looked like a distant photograph in a book. It was so sudden as if, *is this really happening? What now*? I wondered, then Ben's voice, "Mat, you OK?" I gulped, "Yes, yes I think so."

Ahead of us, one to our right and one to our left, I could see our escorts, Cliff and Dan. What a magnificent sight, like floating on a cloud, so smooth! Nothing like the noisy, windy, and bumpy ride in my little bi-plane, *bless her heart. I missed her though.* Ben's voice once more advised, "Hold on, Mat, we are going to do a couple maneuvers." The next thing I remember was doing a giant loop where at the top we leveled off and flew for what seemed like forever, yeh, what else, on our back. Can't describe what that felt like.

Finally we leveled off, thank God, right side up for a while and then did a series of barrel rolls; all I was later told, for this aircraft a very slow speed of only *1000* mph. Ben told me he would have gone faster but was afraid my body wasn't ready for it.... I firmly agreed he was probably right. Our flight lasted about 30 minutes, and it was time to begin our landing approach to

Pawtucket. The plane glided so quiet, like a feather, to a landing and stopped at the point where we had left. To me it seemed eons ago. We climbed down a ladder from our cockpits. I was a bit wobbly but Ben told me it was normal. I almost fainted when he told me that in the short time we had been in flight we logged over 500 miles.

Our two follow planes also landed and Lieutenants Hawes and Molders joined us for our ride back to debriefing, happy to see I had survived. Dr. Alton met us, gave me a once over, and pronounced me in good medical shape.

* * * * *

That was good news, but my senses were still reeling and I was happy this coming afternoon would be easy street. We changed from our flight suits into our duty uniforms and hurried to the command center where Major Dawson met us and advised me that at 1500 I would have a conference with him and the ABC boys.

That was good news as I was anxious to hear what they had to say.

It was now 1330; thus, it didn't leave much time for my command center visit. On the way I told Bill, who had met us upon landing that I had an urgent request for him to arrange for me this evening. "Please invite Sandy on my behalf to dinner this evening at the officers' club and arrange for a private table for two. Use my priority number if you need it, please include a small bouquet of flowers from me, and candles for our table. Tell Sandy I'll pick her up at 1900 hours at her apartment, and please explain I am unable to make this request myself due to important and unavoidable commitments." Bill responded with a smile, "You bet, Mat, it will be my pleasure."

During my command center visit they conducted me through the maze of what they called computers, landing and takeoff radar scopes, radios, GPS monitors, etc. I thought, *Good God, how do they ever make any sense out of it all? All we ever had was a windsock and hand signals.*

Everything dazzled me, but I had a little hands-on fun with some of the amazing machinery, got to talk directly with some pilots, watched planes land on the approach radar scopes, saw them track incoming and outgoing flights, all sorts of wondrous things.

* * * * *

Suddenly it was near 1500 and I hurried to my meeting in Major Dawson's office nearby with the ABC boys. After our usual greetings Major Dawson turned the meeting over to Chaplin Baylor who said, "Lieutenant Mitchell, we have a report from Air Force Personnel. They have located some descendants on your Mathew Mitchell family tree." He handed me the report:

Fred Dale, Son	b.1918	age 82
Fred Dale Jr., Grandson	b.1953	age 47
Lynne Ann, Granddaughter	b.1957	age 43

"Fred Dale Jr., your grandson, is repository for all records of you that have been located. Several photographs of you with Connie, your wife, a few photos of you with your grandparents, a couple photos of you in uniform before departing for France, and your Army Identification Card. And that, Sir, is all they seem to have been able to locate." I reckoned it wasn't a whole lot to remember me by.

Major Dawson interjected, "Mat, would you like us to invite your descendents here for a short reunion?".... That gave me pause to reflect, like *what purpose would it serve? I do not wish to remain here, and they would never understand how I came to show up here in the year 2000 as a much younger person than they were, and then suddenly disappear.* I told Major Dawson I would reflect on his offer, let him know in the morning, and thanked him for his hard work on my behalf. "Now, Gentlemen with your approval I have a very important meeting of my own this evening and have several things to do to get ready. What time should I report back in the morning?" Major Dawson, said, "Go ahead, Mat, enjoy this evening and I'll see you back here at 0930 tomorrow." *I must make my final decision without further delay before tomorrow.* A truly daunting task, but I will have to do it.

Staff Sergeant Bill Karr arrived and we left to pick up Sandy. In addition to finalizing my future plans, I had been thinking concerning tonight. What to talk to Sandy about, what to tell her about my past and my future? Inquire about her life, dance a little even though I am not familiar with any of today's music. Perhaps we might even take a walk in the beautiful moonlight.

We arrived, I knocked on Sandy's door, she opened it, and standing before me was a remarkably beautiful young lady. Charm certainly evidenced itself in more than adequate abundance. I had made a excellent choice for a companion this evening. I helped her into the back seat of our staff car and Sergeant Karr hurried us off to the officers' club where a private table for two with roses and candlelight awaited us. I gallantly held her chair and Sandy sat down. She looked so sweet in the candle glow and softly I said, "Sandy, how delightful you look, so much better by candlelight than in all those bright lights in your office. For a moment these surroundings remind me of how things would kinda look back in 1918." Sandy replied, "Oh, how gallant of you, Mat. I am very complimented, Sir." As we sat the waiter arrived and I ordered a bottle of French Chablis. I continued, "Well, little lady, what shall we talk about? I'd like to hear about now, the year 2000, tell me what your life is all about?"

The waiter returned with our wine, poured a little in my glass, and in the tradition of 1918 I rotated it, sniffed the cork, and replied, "*Il e bon*" (It is good). Then he filled our glasses. Sandy spent the next few minutes telling me about herself, 25 years old, from Pittsburgh, Pennsylvania, college grad, been with the Air Force for three years and plans to make her career in the service.

She then asked, "And now, Mat, you. I am fascinated with what I know of you to-date, 1918 and now 2000; I still can not comprehend this." I answered, "Sandy, I don't really understand it either, one minute I was firing at German planes over France in 1918, and the next I was landing at your airfield here in the year 2000. I have no explanation of this occurrence, but it has certainly left me and everyone else here in a quandary."

After a few minutes of talking about ourselves we ordered our dinners. While we were waiting I asked Sandy to dance to a lovely song called, *Somewhere In Time.* We both commented how appropriate the tune was; from the 1930's it was a bit more my style. I held her close, not inappropriately, and told her how nice it was to be dancing with such a lovely lady. Sandy smiled and held me close. *That was very, very nice*, better than I had hoped for.

After our meal and followed by another glass of wine, I proposed a walk in the moonlight. It was a gracious moon bright evening, and we walked and talked for about an hour. Mostly, at her insistence, about 1918. Seemed she was fascinated by my time travel; thus, I accommodated her. After about a hour we returned to our table for yet a third glass of wine, and some more dancing. Not even once did I make a pass, though it had entered my mind to do so. Fortunately they were only passing thoughts, no more.

By now midnight was approaching and on schedule Bill arrived to pick us up. As it was only a short ride to Sandy's quarters we soon arrived. On the way to her door, I again reiterated how very much I had enjoyed her company and asked if we could do this again? She answered quickly, "Yes, Mat, by all means we can do this again. Whenever you are free, please call me."

I pulled Sandy close to me and kissed her…lightly on the forehead saying, "Goodnight, Sandy, *until next we meet again.*" I was proud of myself this evening, a real gentleman of the old school. Yet I could not help but ask myself, *OK, buddy, but what do you do next?*

* * * * *

Up early, I arrived at 0915 for my 0930 meeting with Major Dawson, Colonel Meyers, and the ABC boys. To my surprise they were already in conference and told me to come in and sit down.

Colonel Meyers, asked if my evening went well and I replied, "Yes, Sir, it was super. Sandy is a truly responsible and lovely young lady, a compliment to the Air Corps." Then I quickly corrected myself, "Excuse me, Sirs, I mean the Service." Everyone laughed.

He continued, "Have you given thought about a small reunion here with your descendents. It would take a little time to arrange it, for as yet we have told no one of your being here, only that we are seeking whatever information they may have relative to your service in France during April 1918. I am certain our inquiries have by themselves stirred their wondering why we are asking about you."

I replied, "Truly, I appreciate your well intentioned offer, Sirs, but *I do not want any reunion.* It would add nothing except confusion and misunderstanding. Further, *I do not plan to remain here in 2000!* I do not belong to this time, and do not wish to remain here. That, Gentlemen, is my decision, and I don't want my family to ever know of my visit here. Is that clear, Sir?" Colonel Meyers, after a short pause, replied, "Yes it is, Lieutenant; although, we had hoped you might have arrived at a different one, we will honor your decision."

Colonel Meyers continued, "Well, Lieutenant, I'm not certain where this leaves us. Obviously we will not consider a reunion, but as for your leaving, what does that mean, to you?" I replied, "Well, Colonel, I am not quite sure, Sir. I am still thinking on it, but leaving does seem to me to be my only real alternative."

Major Dawson nodded, "Gentlemen that pretty much wraps this meeting up. Lieutenant Mitchell, we will need to discuss this more." I agreed, "Yes, and soon, Sir." I stood, saluted, turned, and left his office. I walked straight to the officers' club, went to the bar, and over the next couple of hours lost myself in thought over a few glasses of wine.

Well that was it. Now to implement my attempt at leaving, and if successful where will it take me? I thought and thought until finally my plan was formulated and knew with absolute confidence what to do. By noon, my head was clear. Having worked everything out, tomorrow morning I would do it.

But first I wanted to talk to Captain Ben Morris; thus, I called and asked him to meet me here at the club for lunch which he readily agreed to do. After lunch I said, "Ben, I have a job involving a trip to Arizona. During my stay here Colonel Meyers and his staff identified my ancestors and wanted to bring some of them here for a reunion.

"I turned the reunion idea down flat. However, I have put together a few items which I would like for you to take to my son, Fred Dale Mitchell, who now resides in Mesa,

Arizona. The items are my wings, my identification tag, my lieutenants bars, a couple of photographs of me and my wife taken just before leaving for France. Perhaps I can replace some of these items later. Ben, will you do this for me?"

He replied, "Of course, Mat, but why don't you do this yourself?" I answered, "Because, Ben, there is no way to explain why I am here. Hell, I can't even explain it to myself. Please, this is my irrevocable decision, will you do this for me, no more questions asked?" After a short pause he said he would go. I stood, again saluted, said, "Thank you, my friend. I will be eternally grateful. Here are the items you are to take." I saluted him once more, smiled, said, "See you around," did an about face and left the club.

* * * * *

In the afternoon, I walked over to the hanger where my plane was parked under a canopy. I knew she was fueled and serviced in accordance with Major Dawson's orders, and she looked ready for flight. I had checked the weather for tomorrow, partly cloudy and warm. *Nice day for a plane ride*, I thought.

I returned to my quarters, showered, and later returned to the officers' club for a light meal, a couple drinks, and some deep thought, mostly of Connie and Sandy. I wished to see them once more, but of course that was only a pipe dream and it made me hurt inside. At 2200 I retired, hoping for a few winks before my room call would arrive at 0500.

Fortune smiled and I slept rather soundly until my telephone rang. Then dressed in my ancient flight uniform, I drank some juice and milk left in my refrigerator, and at 0630 headed to my plane. As I approached she looked so beautiful, her lines familiar in every aspect. She was sitting in an access area headed downwind as if expecting I would come, and was ready for whatever was about to happen.

* * * * *

I reached inside the cockpit, switched on the ignition switch, walked to the front of my plane, and began to prime the engine with a couple turns of the prop. Then with a high leg kick gave the prop a hard downward thrust. My plane's engine sputtered, then fired smoothly. I kicked her wheel chucks free and hurried to get into the cockpit.

As I did I saw a staff car racing toward me. It screeched to a stop beside my plane and Major Dawson ran to the side of my cockpit with his pistol drawn and pointed at my head. He yelled, "Lieutenant, turn off your engine and get out of your plane right now!" I replied, "Sir, let's not go through all this again. With all due respect you have my permission to go ahead and shoot."

I immediately released my brakes and with my throttle open my little plane began to roll. Major Dawson, of course, did not shoot, and as I began my roll in the distance I could see him salute me. Shortly my Sopwith

Camel was airborne and the ground, buildings, and people slowly receded and finally disappeared in the distance. I felt a sense of freedom and headed my plane east toward a cloud bank above me.

Major Dawson rushed back to his control center where they were tracking my departure. He was immediately asked if chase planes should be sent aloft to intercept and immediately he said, "No, let him go, just keep him on radar."

I entered the cloud bank, leveled off at 7500 feet, and headed due east out over the ocean. There was nothing now for me to do except fly and think. So far my plan was working as I hoped it would; simply fly due east until either something happened, or if nothing did, to dive my little plane into the ocean below. I simply wished not to remain as an apparition in the year 2000.

* * * * *

Back at the center everyone, including Sandy, was watching my plane's small blip on a radar monitor. My distance was increasing, first to 50 miles, then 60, and at 100 miles my blip began to slowly fade from their screen.

A few minutes later the radar officer in charge said, "*Sir, he is gone.*" Major Dawson stood silently for several moments before replying, "No, Gentlemen, Lieutenant Mitchell is not gone for he is a *whiffenpoof*.... A little black sheep who has lost his way, and may God have mercy on his soul for he is doomed to roam the skies for all eternity. He is now in the company of gentlemen songsters off on a spree, their songs to be heard by pilots, flying alone, lost in the sky on some cold and dreary night. No, don't ever feel sorry for him. We should all salute his memory for he is a true hero."

The center remained stealthily quiet for several moments until Captain Morris stood, saluted, and everyone followed his lead. Captain Morris said, "Three cheers, Lieutenant Mathew Mitchell, US Army Flying Squadron Number 26, from this day on my plane will always be called, *The Whiffenpoof.*

* * * * *

Meanwhile, I had now flown about 150 miles and began to lower myself below my cloud cover in anticipation. If I did not find land I would nose my plane into the ocean, about three minutes below. By now my mind had entered an euphoric state of emotional well being. My only surviving thoughts were of my wife, Connie, and my son who according to Chaplin Baylor had just been born. I would never be able to tell Connie nor my son goodbye or tell them how much I love them.

Moments later my plane cleared the clouds.... *I saw below me not ocean...only land!* My heart jumped and began to beat harder.... *Land, but not just any land,* it looked very much like the area around Cerlot? Could it be I have completed some sort of a cycle and returned to the exact place and time that I had left? Yes, yes... *look over there...it's my airfield... it's Cerlot, I'd know it anywhere.*

Excitedly, with my heart beating wildly, I banked sharply and began my descent, switching my engine off and on creating that familiar, *bluurp, bluurp, blurp*. It sounded so good to me. Suddenly my wheels touched ground and I could see the other planes of Squadron 26 lined up neatly near their hangers. As my plane taxied to where they were, I cut my engine and rolled to a stop.

Leaping from my cockpit I was surrounded immediately by everyone, my fellow pilots, Major Taylor, Sergeant Dubois, and the rest of the maintenance crew. I had landed a couple hours later than the others, and was assumed to be down someplace. Dubois called, "Where have you been?"

A reasonable question and certainly one for which I had no reasonable answer. So I chuckled, "Oh, shit, I got lost, yeh, lost and chased all over hell's half acre. It was like the entire German Luftwaffe was after me. Got me another Heine, but I have no confirmation on it."

* * * * *

Everything quickly settled back into a familiar routine. I had received a letter from Connie dated April 26, 1918 telling me I was the father of a bouncing baby boy named Frederick after his grandfather and Dale after his father, and hoped that all was OK with me. I immediately mailed her a letter telling her yes, absolutely, and that I love you both very much with every inch of my soul. Please take care and I will do the same. Can't wait to see you.

Over the following couple months I had mostly recovered from my escapade to the year 2000. Since I had only been gone a couple hours Cerlot time, things remained as they had. Squadron 26 continued to fly sorties about four times each week. During May I claimed three more kills, but we lost two pilots, 2nd Lieutenants Abbott (killed), and Purvis (taken prisoner). Our total squadron kill total for May was eleven, not too bad. Replacements for Abbott and Pervis arrived on June 4th, Jimmy Lee Hart and Collin Kelly. Both new pilots who would need to receive advance training before they enter combat.

Since returning my mind often raced back to Pawtucket, Delaware, to Captain Ben Morris, Major Dawson, and to Sandy Greer. Between sorties I wrote letters to Connie, mom and dad, and thought often of Sandy. I was so happy to have a photo of her which I kept along side Connie's. Somehow, under these circumstances I didn't think either of them would mind.

On 6 June, Major Taylor summoned me and CW to his headquarters and informed us of a busy schedule for all squadrons beginning 8 June. There would be maximum efforts all along the front. Evidently an enemy offensive was underway, and we were to perform strafing and bombing raids on all targets of opportunity along our

front lines. That would mean four planes in pairs would do the strafing and bombing while the other two planes would fly cover. I assigned CW and 2nd Lieutenant, Billy the Kidd, Kane to fly cover while I would lead the others on the raiding passes. Takeoff time on 8 June would be 0545.

8 June was not a great day weather wise, cloudy, misty, and ground temperature a cool 55F degrees. With the wind chill it felt more like 40F, but we were bundled up for it. Our flying time to the target area was estimated at twenty-five minutes.

At 0530 our planes were fired up and ready to roll. Sergeant Dubois gave us the closed fist above the head sign. I raised my hand and the others followed suit, and as I dropped my hand, all six planes in unison began their roll. As usual we took off in twos, climbed rapidly to 4,000 feet, in formation according to our assignments, and were on our way.

Even with the cold wind rushing across my cockpit I still felt the elegance of flying that even this deadly war could not diminish. The majesty of flying was still so new it gave one a feeling of object superiority.

Soon, there they were. Separated by about 300 yards opposing trenches stretched to the north and south as far as the eye could see. They looked like nasty squirming snakes and between them the land was pock marked by shell craters, barbed wire, and debris of all sorts. Truly it was what it was called, *no-man's-land.* If I had to be a part of this horrific struggle, I was glad to be up here where the air was fresh and I wasn't buried up to my knees in water and slime.

As we approached, I raised my arm and waved it back-and- forth, the signal to attack. CW and Billy roared to gain altitude and take their positions covering us from unsuspected attacks by German fighters. I waved my arm downward and the remaining four of us split into two groups and headed for the giant convoy of trucks carrying supplies to feed the new offensive. There was no difficulty in finding targets.

We roared full throttle down the line of vehicles at about 200 feet altitude, and our twin 30 caliber machine guns spat out their lethal pellets. I could see them striking home and men were falling from the vehicles; explosions, fire, and smoke filled the air. We were causing some real carnage and mayhem within the enemy ranks.

However, it wasn't without resistance. We were taking intense ground fire from many anti-aircraft machine guns mounted on trucks. I glanced upward and caught a quick sighting of CW and Billy engaged and outnumbered by several Fokkers. A thought raced through my mind, *Good Lord, bless us all for we may never see the light of day again, but we will do our best.*

We managed our first pass without losing anyone, but we had taken hits. Our four planes quickly made a 180 degree turn and flew back in the opposite direction along the same line of vehicles. We would complete the strafing run and continue directly back to our base at Cerlot.

About midway through the strafing run, Mitchell's ship was hit and caught fire, immediately exploded, and at full speed plowed into the ground along side of the convoy. Lieutenant John Henry Dowd, his wingman for the day, upon landing reported to Major Taylor, saying, "Lieutenant Mitchell could never have survived the crash, Sir." Second Lieutenant Jimmy Lee Hart, one of the new pilots, was also lost. He was the trailing plane in the squadron's formation and no one saw him go down. Squadron 26 had lost two of their six planes, including their squadron commander. Not at all an unusual result of such a contact with the enemy.

The next day, a lone German plane over flew the Cerlot aerodrome and dropped a package containing Mitchell's helmet and goggles, his wristwatch, his wedding band, and identification tag. Also it included a note stating Lieutenant Mitchell's body had been recovered and he was buried in the church graveyard at Lemont, a small village about 40 miles west of Cerlot.

No report from the Germans was received on 2nd Lieutenant Jimmy Lee Hart. His family was later notified by Major Taylor that he was listed as missing in action and presumed dead, that his loss would be noted among the bravest of Squadron 26's fallen. A stark and sudden testament to a young American's life so suddenly gone.

At least Connie was the recipient of a more informative letter from Major Taylor. A package arrived on July 10th which contained both a personal letter from Mathew and his personal effects: United States Air Corps identification tag, a wristwatch, wedding band, a photo of him and Connie, wallet including $17.00, and a letter which read:

My dearest Connie and Freddy. Should you ever receive this letter, know I have no regrets of dying for my country and the liberties we all cherish. I am eternally happy you and Freddy will always remember me as a soldier of democracy, and my love will travel with you into eternity. I love you both.... Mat

Next was a hand written letter from Major Taylor, cosigned by 2nd Lieutenant Charles (CW) London, Mat's wingman and friend. It read:

Dear Connie: It is with unimaginable grief that CW and I write this letter to you. In the short time we were to know Mat, our admiration for his honesty, bravery and devotion to duty was never in question. His total of 4 German planes and uncountable other enemy assets destroyed were a significant accomplishment, not to mention his leadership of Squadron 26 here at Cerlot, France. Mat always thought of himself as a *Whiffenpoof*, roaming the skies for all time. We never did really understand what he meant, but he knew, and we are certain he is doing his thing now.

Connie, should either of us return from this war, and are able to do so, we will look you up. With our fondest respect, we enclose a copy of the note dropped onto our airfield by the Germans which details the burial location of Mat's remains.... We wish you well.

Signed: Rob and CW

* * * * *

July 10,1918, the day Connie prayed and prayed would not happen, happened, and only her three month old son, Freddy, was there to comfort her. Connie was a very composed young lady and not subject to overly emotional exhibitions, but this was beyond her control, and she had to share this terrible news with someone.

Mat's parents lived only a couple blocks away; thus, she grabbed Freddy and rushed to their house. As she entered it was obvious bad news had arrived, and she was only able to hand Mat's parents the items she had just received. Obviously they were stunned at the suddenness of this news. After awhile, talking back-and-forth helped. As with Connie, it was something they had hardened themselves to…the possibility that Mat would never come home. Time crept by ever so slowly, but eventually in time memories began to fade.

Connie did not have a job; thus, she moved in with Mat's folks who were comforted by the fact that Freddy was every bit their little Mat. In 1921 Connie remarried an Army veteran named Henry Cox. Henry was a fine man and had a good job as an installer with the Illinois Bell Telephone Company. They were blessed with two children, Martha, born 1923, and Harry, born 1924. Time moved ceaselessly on.

PART 2

FRED - ANOTHER LIFE GOES ON

1918-2000

During the years 1924 to 1938 I graduated from Harvard Park Grade School, Springfield High School, and Springfield Junior College. I was a B plus average student, lettering in such sports as basketball, track, football, and baseball.

During those years I had grown up hearing about my father's exploits as a fighter pilot during WWI, shooting down four German planes before he was killed in action during a strafing sortie in 1918. It seemed a rather foregone conclusion that I would follow in my father's footsteps. Although I wanted to join the army, much to my mother's relief, I had no ambition to be a flier.

In the summer of 1939 I enlisted in the Army and in accordance with my request was posted to the infantry training facility at Fort Bliss, Texas. After completing basic training I was assigned to a mechanized scout squad whose purpose was to patrol ahead of advancing army units. I was pleased, as it seemed to be a challenging assignment.

By the time the war began in December 1941, I had advanced to the rank of corporal, in charge of one of our squad's two man automatic rifle (bar) teams. Soon thereafter our outfit left Texas for advanced training at a desolate and sun soaked newly established Desert Training Center located near Indio, California.

Following our training we were assigned as a unit in General George S. Patton's newly activated First Armored Corps. Thus, we would soon become a part of

Operation Torch, code name for the invasion of North Africa.

My squad was assigned to Captain David Barrows, Company A of the First Regiment, Third Division, of number Three Corps. Everyone was excited about the prospects of an early entry into WWII and we weren't disappointed.

In late summer 1942 we landed on the coast of Vichy French Morocco and immediately were engaged on the beach by French and Moroccan troops. However, the battle was short lived and we were soon accepted by the French as allies, rather than foes, which made us all quite happy.

As we proceeded east our squad became engaged by well trained and well armed German panzers. And as point scouts we were quickly overwhelmed and had to fall back. Nevertheless, my automatic rifle team destroyed an armored vehicle and killed several German troopers, which for awhile stalled the enemy attack, thus permitting a safe withdrawal of several forward units. I was commended by our Division commander and promoted to sergeant.

My good luck lasted for only three days, when again we encountered strong German resistance during a panzer attack. I received a serious shrapnel wound in my left shoulder which required being removed to a field hospital, and finally evacuated back to the states for mending.

After a lengthy recovery at Brooke Army Medical Center in San Antonio, Texas, which included a considerable physical therapy program, I was returned to the Indio, California Infantry Training Center and assigned to training new mechanized recon squads…and promoted to second lieutenant. Suddenly, I was now an officer and a gentleman.

I liked my job, was good at it, and remained at the Indio training facility until my discharge from the Army in late 1945 as a first lieutenant. After my discharge I enlisted in the Army Reserve, and remained at Springfield, Illinois until June 1950 when the Korean War broke out and my reserve unit, the 468th Field Artillery Battalion, was called back to active duty.

Because of my wounds from WWII, accompanied by an increased demand for trained reconnaissance units, I was once again assigned to training recon units at the Indio, California training facility. I remained there until my release from active duty and returned to Army Reserve status in November 1951. My official and final discharge from the Army as a First Lieutenant took place in Springfield on 13 June, 1953.

I had joined Illinois Bell Telephone Company on December 1, 1951, and at the age of 34, married Shirley Rhea Thorndal, age 22, on June 14, 1952. We had two children, Fred Jr., born 1953, and Lynne Ann born 1957. In November 1974 I was transferred to A T & T in New York and later New Jersey until my retirement to Arizona in November 1984.

During my retirement years I pursued my avocations, Military History, particularly the American Civil War, World Wars I and II, Duplicate Bridge, travel, cruising, and golf.

* * * * *

In the summer of 1968 Shirley and I watched on television a one hour special, the visit of German General Hasso von Manteuffel to President Dwight D. Eisenhower's estate at Gettysburg, Pennsylvania. They discussed in detail the Battle of the Bulge which had taken place at Bastogne in Belgium during the Christmas season of 1944.

What a fit! Shirley and I had planned our first of what would become several trips to Germany and France to specifically study WWI and WWII battles along the Western Front. In France I especially wanted to visit

Cerlot aerodrome and Lemont where my father was buried. I quickly wrote General von Manteuffel at his home in Diessen am Ammersee near Munich. I really didn't expect a reply; however, in less than two weeks one arrived typed in very good English:

Dear Fred and Madame Mitchell:

Frau Manteuffel and I will be most pleased to have you visit us. Please call us when you arrive in the area. *Besten Grusse* (Best Greetings).

Hasso von Manteuffel, General der Panzertruppen

Of course Shirley and I immediately accepted his invitation. In May 1969, from the Landsberger Inn at Landsburg near Diessen, we called General von Manteuffel and were invited to visit his home the next day. I was so excited that I worried all night about what to say. Finally, I decided just being myself was my best hope. As we arrived, I presented Frau Manteuffel with a small bouquet of flowers, saying, "*Gnadige Frau, Fur Ihnen*" (Madame, for you). I was an instant hit.

My frantic concerns of last evening soon evaporated. I was adequately prepared, and General and Frau von Manteuffel were gracious hosts and very easy to talk with. Our meeting lasted for over three hours during which time Frau von Manteuffel showed us about their home and offered us a glass of excellent German wine. Of course General von Manteuffel and I spent most of the time discussing details of the Battle of the Bulge.

Upon closing our visit, the General offered he would be pleased to answer any other questions I might have via post, and I heartily thanked him. Also he said, "Herr Mitchell, you remind somewhat of an American lieutenant I once had the pleasure of meeting while he was my prisoner during the battle." I thought, *An interesting comment. It seemed unusual he would have a meeting with an American lieutenant under such circumstances. Perhaps someday I'll have the opportunity to ask him more of that encounter.* (Editors Note: I had not yet experienced the actual battle (in my current timeline), though of course the General had.)

Shirley and I said our thanks and goodbyes and as we left Diessen said to Shirley, "I'll sure stay in touch with the General and when we return to Germany we'll be certain to visit again and hopefully stay longer."

We left Diessen and drove into France on the way to Cerlot where my father was stationed in 1918. Cerlot was approximately 150 miles from Diessen. The following morning we would visit dad's grave at Lemont.

When we arrived at Cerlot we booked two nights at a small, lovely, and quaint Inn named Le Cerlot. The Innkeeper, Monsieur Benoit, fortunately spoke some English. Not much, but it helped and to the mix, Shirley added her knowledge of a few French words. Monsieur Benoit was able to direct us to where the aerodrome was located and during the afternoon we visited there.

I don't know what I expected, but it was disappointing. The old aerodrome was...dilapidated. The past fifty-one years had not been kind. Several old worn buildings some of which were at one time hangers, a tower for observing returning planes, what once might have been a barracks and mess hall, some junky remains of engines, wheels, and other unidentifiable stuff were littered about.

The runways were overgrown with about two foot high grass swaying in the breeze as if being propelled by the propeller blasts from many airplanes just waiting to take off into battle.

Yes, yes, I could hear them, their engines roaring as they began their race down the runway. The smell of engine oil was pervasive. I asked Shirley, "Honey, do you hear them?" She only looked quietly at me; of course, she didn't hear them, but she knew that I did. Yes I did see them....Then, it was him, I saw him!...*Dad in his cockpit, his plane just beginning it's roll....* Only for a moment and soon he was gone, with his entire squadron, disappearing like specters into the distance of time.

Everything returned to normal, *but it had seemed so real.* The grass was once more blowing gently in the breeze… the planes and smells, they were all gone.

* * * * *

The next morning after a delightful breakfast at the Inn we left for Lemont, a distance of about 40 miles from Cerlot. It was a lovely small village and we had no difficulty locating the ancient church where the cemetery was located. There was no one around to assist us so we just started looking. Soon we came upon an area where several WWI graves were located and we found dad's marker. It was a nice granite stone:

Mathew Dale Mitchell, 1st Lieutenant
26th Squadron, United States Air Corps
8 June, 1918

It was an extremely emotional moment. We stood there quietly for some time. Shirley took my hand saying, "Fred, I am so proud to be here with you." I answered,

"Thank you, honey." And with emotion continued, "Dad, on behalf of your grandchildren, Connie, Shirley and myself we love you and are very, very proud of you. We, and our entire country, owe you and all your brave comrades so much."

Our visit to Europe had now been completed and we continued our drive back to Luxemburg City where we boarded our Icelandic Air flight home. Our trip was a prelude to several more visits we would make to call upon General von Manteuffel and his lovely wife.

* * * * *

As the years continued… from 1984 to the year 2000 I was able, with the help my friend, an angel named Bob, to take a couple trips back in time. First to be onboard the Hindenburg on her fatal flight from Germany to New Jersey in May 1937, and the second to December 7, 1941 as a participant in the Japanese attack on Pearl Harbor, Hawaii.

Bob was an itinerate old cowboy who lost his life on the western trails back in the 1880's and became an angel working with time travelers such as me. I first met Bob at my favorite watering hole in Tortilla Flat, Arizona.

* * * * *

Why am I having a premonition that I will soon be seeing Bob again?

PART 3

ANOTHER TIME

2000

In the desert near Tortilla Flat on this day, this lovely day in May of the year 2000, I sit relaxing on my camp stool enjoying the magnificent sights and the subtle sounds of the desert, a routine which I have often done throughout my retirement. It is a day perfect for meditation, a day when random thoughts can unconstrained crisscross the channels of my mind.

Without warning my mind once more zoned in on thinking about my previous escapades back in time: to 1937, the Hindenburg on her fatal trip from Germany to New Jersey, and my participation during the infamous

December 7th, 1941 Japanese attack on our fleet at Pearl Harbor, Hawaii.

Just sitting and thinking of the excitement of these journeys led me to ponder, *would it be possible for me to take one more trip back in time?* My mind suddenly made a mid course correction. My wife, Shirley, would either kill me or leave me, and neither of those alternatives were attractive. At my age, forget it.... But wait!... *unless...yes, maybe? Hell yes, what does age have to do with it? Hell yes, I can do it!*

When I traveled back in time to Pearl Harbor, I did so as a 44 year old Commander in the Navy...and the resulting nine day trip only required me to be away from my current time for about 5 hours.... Oh, *wonders of wonders...*would Bob, the angel who made my Hindenburg and Pearl Harbor trips in time possible, ever champion another trip for me? I continued to ponder. *Where would I go? How long would I be away? Could I actually once more revert to a younger me? How would I handle Shirley?*

* * * * *

After awhile it was time to leave the desert and make an appearance at Big John's bar in Tortilla Flat for a large frothy stein of Irish ale. As I entered the saloon Big John and his son, Little John, were both in attendance. Although Big John had "retired" he still spent much of his time mingling with the pack, exchanging jokes as if he was aware the bar's ambience wasn't the same without his being there.

When John saw me enter he exclaimed in his broadest Irish brogue, "Freddy, darlin', to be certain it be good to see ya." I smiled, waved, took a seat at the bar where Martha, my favorite barmaid, shoved a tall one in front of me and rewarded me with one of her great smiles. I said, "Martha, me beauty, I be forever holden to ye." As Big John and I frequently did we bantered back and forth chatting about my time travel escapades as he called them. He had always been fascinated with discussing them, and as usual the subject turned to *Crazy* Bob, who I met at Big John's bar several years ago and who guided me on my last two trips back in time.

Bob got his name *Crazy* because of the way he dressed in old style cowboy attire, and his hermit-like demeanor. John never got over meeting him and I didn't dare tell him of my thinking about taking another venture. Although I loved Big John like a brother, I could not tell him anything in advance of it happening. Not so much that he wasn't trustworthy, but he would drive me nuts with questions. After about an hour it was go home time and on the way my mind continued to churn. *What should I say to Shirley, to Bob, and specifically where do I want to go and what do I want to do?*

Over the course of the following week I returned a couple of times to the desert to think and develop a more detailed plan, and importantly, how to go about finding Bob?

After a lot of thought I returned home to my library and computer room. I poured through my books and researched Wikipedia. At last, since my Pearl Harbor trip was so successful, a destination began to materialize.... I would opt for a trip back to WWII in Europe as a younger person.

I continued to think and eventually a plan began to take shape. I would join General George S. Patton's 3rd Army as a 26 year old infantry first lieutenant, trained in motorized reconnaissance, protecting General Patton's flanks as he moved from Normandy to Metz in France, then moving with a large portion of his Third Army north to relieve the American troops encircled at Bastogne, Belgium in December 1944. This would be an interesting assignment and one where I could utilize my training and experiences during the war in North Africa as a sergeant with a similar group of men.

But now, how to contact Bob? I considered, *just do as you had done before*. Return to the same place in the desert near Tortilla Flat where previously you contacted him before your trip to Pearl Harbor. I said to myself, *Well, of course, dummy, seems reasonable.*

* * * * *

The next morning I returned to that barren, sandy, rocky, and very still place in the desert near Tortilla Flat. Nothing here stood between me and isolation except saguaro cacti, a few mesquite trees, arroyos, and the mountains and lakes in the distance. It was so strangely beautiful, and it certainly provided me with plenty of privacy and solitude.

I sat down on my camp stool, crossed my fingers, and quietly announced, "*Bob, Bob, it's me, Fred, I need you.*" After five minutes of waiting, nothing. I said, in a louder voice, *"Bob, Bob, where the heck are you, ole friend?"* Still nothing, like always, I guessed he just wanted to make things a little difficult. *Why does he always do this to me?* I took a swig of cool water from my canteen, waited, and waited. The sun was warm and I was a little tired.

I wiped the sweat from my brow, and hollered louder, *"BOB! I have suffered enough!"*

Suddenly there was this feeling like something or someone was standing behind me. I slowly turned and sure enough there he was. A short distance away stood the sights I had been waiting for. The giant mesquite tree, the little shack, and in the doorway leaning against an open door was Bob.

What a relief! Bob said, "Hello, Fred, good to see ya, come in, been waiten long? I can hardly wait to hear whatcha got in mind this time, ole pal." I smiled, "Hello, Bob, boy it's good to see you too."

He led me inside the little shack; it was almost like a feeling of returning home as this was my third visit here. As always, there was only a candle and some light entering via a small window and the open door. It sure wasn't much, but it was familiar and did feel comfortable.

"Fred, please sit yer self down; didn't expect to see ya here so soon." I replied, cutting right to the facts, "Yes, Bob, this has to be a surprise, but I want to take one more trip." .... After what seemed a long delay he answered, "Yikes, hadn't counted on that, Fred, ya sure that be what ya want?"

My reply was simple, "Yes, Bob, it is. Since you have guided me on two previous journeys, I now want to go to Europe and again be a part of the war in 1944. As you know, I did participate in northern Africa during that war in 1942, and now I want to go back to be with Patton as he pushes from Normandy to Metz in France and then north to Bastogne in Belgium. And I have some specifics in mind."

Bob, answered, "Yes, I know." *I had forgotten he always knows my mind, sometimes even before I have decided on something.* I added, "Is there any need for me to ask about specifics of what I want to do?" He continued, "No, don't think so, Fred. Let's see, it's August 1, 1944, 26 years old, first lieutenant, reconnaissance squad,

General Patton's Third Army, France. Do I have it right?" I responded, "As usual, Sir, you do." Bob continued, "Then, Fred, I have but one question at this time. Are ya ready to go?" My reply again was simple, "I'll be at this place, right here, one week from today, if that is okay?"

Bob answered, "That be good, old buddy, I'll have everything you'll need ready. See ya here at 7:30 AM a week from today. Say, hello, to Shirley for me." Shirley had met Bob after my last trip during a lunch at Big John's. She had never known in advance about my previous trips and now do I tell her about this one? Thought to myself.... *Nope not right now, later for sure.*

Now I had but two major things to do. Get Shirley on a visit to see the children, which I arranged for. Second, finalize the specifics of my plan. The following week moved ahead quickly as I continued to refine my thinking and Shirley left for her family visit.

* * * * *

My "D" Day was here! At 7:30 AM I parked my car near Tortilla Flat and walked into the desert to where Bob would hopefully be waiting. It was a delightful morning, this morning in May. As I walked over a small rise a short distance away the little shack appeared and beside it stood the large mesquite tree; both were sights I was by now used to seeing, but no Bob was present. I was not surprised.

I walked up to the door, knocked, and echoing his dialect said, "Bob, I be here, are ya here?" Moments passed, before the door opened and Bob stepped outside. "Mornin', my friend. It be good to see ya. Come ye in and sit down, Fred, and I'll be coverin' the ground rules for ye trip fast as ye have been through them before. The *Train to Perpetuity* will arrive shortly, and as she has done before will take ye where ye have chosen to be agoin'.

"Like on the last trips everything ye will need is ready, but I remind ye again that ye cain't significantly change history or the trip be immediately aborted as if it had ne're happened." I just shook my head. God, I love this guy. *Crazy*, he is referred to by some, but *Crazy* he ain't, itinerant, he ain't! He just be Bob, my friend, angel, and mentor.

Soon I heard the *Train to Perpetuity approaching,* her whistle blaring as she neared. We went outside and there she stood, belching smoke like a mad snake from her old fashioned smokestack, tooting her whistle, and hissing steam which poured from her boilers like clouds of hot breath on a cold winter morning.

As always, a coal tender and one passenger coach were attached. The conductor got off, placed a step stool for Bob and me to use, and the engineer and fireman were in their usual place in the *Train's* cab. It came as no surprise to me that they looked like the same people who took me on my last two trips. Yes, I am positive that they were.

We got on board and as always the conductor shouted, "All aboard" *to nobody* and waved his lantern. After a sudden lurch, as if in chorus, I heard the chug, chug, chug, clang, clang, clang, hiss, hiss, hiss as the *Train to Perpetuity* began her journey on our way back in time to the year 1944.

Each time I witnessed this event I just shook my head. What an unusual conveyance the *Perpetuity* is for transporting one into the fourth dimension! But as Bob so apply puts it, "Whatcha expect, a speed boat?"

* * * * *

I sat back in my seat and watched the scenery rush by my window as it evaporated into a bluish blur as we began to cross time continuums. Bob came by and said, "Seen this before, huh?" I retorted, "Yes, Sir, I have, but I never get used to it."

Bob continued, "Fred as we always do, we'll be stoppin' for about an hour to help you adjust to 1944. This time it will be at 1944 Jacksonville, Illinois. With all your experiences on the *Hindenburg*, at *Pearl Harbor*, and north Africa, this foray should be a cakewalk for you." He grinned and zestfully added, "But we'll stop anyway, ole buddy." I thought, *Jacksonville, Illinois, I have a lot of memories tucked away in Jacksonville.* My family actually lived there for a few months before returning to Springfield. However, in only one hour I won't be able to see much.

As I sat and contemplated my visit, the conductor arrived with my dress uniform, my M-1, and a good sized mirror. Bob continued, "Here, Fred, get into your uniform and take a look at the new you. After I was dressed Bob handed me the mirror and as I looked in it I was startled to see me, a good looking young army first lieutenant. "Looks good, Fred, how's 26 go fer ya?" I smiled, "OK by me, Bob, I was an *old* man of 44 at Pearl and I got around there in pretty good shape." He chuckled, "Yup," and continued, "we'll soon be ah stoppen in Jacksonville."

As the train hissed, squealed and poured off smoke we came to rest in front of the depot. I got off and was not surprised; it was obvious no one could see neither me nor the train… until I had walked away some 50 yards. Then people began to notice me in my uniform; they seemed genuinely appreciative.

I figured, the only thing now was take a cab and drive by familiar places that would bring back memories of the short time I lived here as a youth. The cabby was pleased to act as my guide. We drove by the place where we lived on Beecher Street, past the grade school I attended, then made a short stop at Mac Murray college from where Shirley will graduate in 1952. Finally we stopped at the town square; I walked around it once. People cordially greeted me and I smiled back; it was a rather eerie feeling, but nice. Now my hour was up and I returned to where Bob and the *Train to Perpetuity* stood awaiting me, again invisible to all, except to me. We boarded the *Train* and were soon chugging our way toward 1944 France.

* * * * *

Bob told me we would arrive in France in about two hours, and after that I would be on my own. Guess I knew the script; thus, we sat down to get me ready.

The conductor laid out my battle fatigues and other equipment that included a supply of 30 caliber ammunition for my M-1. Then Bob handed me my official US Army travel orders, thirty dollars in 1944 money, and explained where and to whom I should report. My sense of anticipation had reached its zenith.

Bob looked at me and said, "Don't ya ever git tired o' doin' this stuff?" I smiled, and responded, "Well, not really. How else can I enjoy so much excitement at my age?" He grinned a toothy smile and simply said, "Yeh!" I just smiled back…and thought, *He truly does look as if he just stepped from a Grant Wood painting.*

The *Train to Perpetuity* would pause *unseen* while I disembarked. It was a short walk to Third Army

Headquarters, where I would report to Captain Charles N. Horne, C Company, 6th Recon Battalion. From that time on until my visit to 1944 was over I would be on my own. There would be no one to help me. For some reason I wasn't the least bit nervous. Guess there's something to be said for, *been there, done that.* I certainly hoped my courage would continue; for certain I would soon find out.

PART 4

A DAMN COLD DECEMBER

FRANCE - WESTERN FRONT, 1944

On the Moselle River near Metz, France First Lieutenant Fred D. Mitchell US Army is attached to General George S. Patton's Third Army as a reconnaissance (recon) officer. His specialty will be to command a motorized picket line along General Patton's flanks, or as required, in the lead of varied infantry and armored units. It was 1 August 1944 when I reached the headquarters of Captain Charles Nelson Horne, commanding officer of C Company, 6th Reconnaissance Battalion, 3'rd US Army.

I was quickly assigned as commanding officer of Recon 1 composed of three jeeps: (lead vehicle) a staff sergeant, corporal and two riflemen, (second vehicle) myself, radioman, and one rifleman, and (third vehicle) sergeant, two riflemen, and a medical corporal. I speak adequate German and Staff Sergeant Dieter Troutner, my second in command, is fluent.

Fortunately, from the advantage point of time, I had studied Patton's movements following the Normandy invasion. From the early fighting in Normandy during August, Third Army spearheaded the allies advances during the late stages of Operation Cobra (the breakout into France).

Patton's Third Army simultaneously attacked west into Brittany, south and east towards the Seine River, and northward, where it assisted in trapping thousands of German soldiers in the Chambois pocket between Falaise and Argentan.

Continuing our advance to Argentan, Patton, rather than continually engaging in close order slugging matches, applied many of the tenets of the Germans' own blitzkrieg war. He utilized all elements of the American Army, including the Air Corps, during his 60 mile thrust.

However just outside Metz on 31 August near the Moselle River, Third Army's rapid advance ended. Patton had outrun his supply lines while exploiting a German weakness, their mobility. Now he was stuck in Alsace-Lorraine and the cutback in our offensive capabilities enabled the Germans to re-supply, rest, and strengthen their fortifications in and around Metz.

During the slow down my life and the activities of my squad were comparatively quiet. We enjoyed ten days of rest and relaxation in the lovely countryside along the Moselle River. This meant clean clothing, daily showers, good hot food, USO shows, movies, beer, dances, and girls, girls, girls. It seemed this was the order of the day. We laughed, "Now this is what war should be." We were languishing in the Western Fronts definition of the lap of luxury and loving every moment of it.

However our respite from the war didn't last forever and it ended on September 15th when after receiving fresh supplies Third Army once more began to move. Slowly, at first, as advance units began probing the defenses of Metz itself. Our small group of eleven intrepid soldiers, known as Recon 1, was assigned scouting Third Army's northern flank, probing several miles beyond American lines to seek out German presence, their numbers and strength (panzers, artillery, etc.).

Reconnoitering is not a task meant for sissies. My group of experienced and highly trained men consisted of:

First Lieutenant Fred Mitchell
Staff Sergeant Dieter Troutner
Sergeant Wayne Marcello
Corporal Ben Crawford
Corporal Harry Temple (Medic)
Private First Class Frank Caesar

Private First Class Chris Ford (Radioman)
Private Donald Bell
Private Anson Purdy
Private Gene Kelly
Private Burt Hepburn

* * * * *

Finally, fortress Metz surrendered to Third Army on 23 November, but Recon 1's patrolling and picketing activities continued unabated. While on patrol during a rather cold 26 November we approached a magnificent chateau. As we neared we saw a sign on a large iron entry gate which read, *Chateau Bellevue.*

We had not seen any indications of German activity in the vicinity, but I decided that a look around was called for. It was unlikely the Germans would have passed this place without a stopover of some kind. Also it seemed strange that no one appeared to be around.

Thus, I ordered Sergeant Marcello, Privates Hepburn and Purdy to check the chateau's outer buildings, told Corporal Crawford, Private First Class Caesar, Radioman Private First Class Ford, and Medic Corporal Temple to stay with the vehicles while Privates Bell and Kelly were picketed respectively about 100 yards to our north and south. Staff Sergeant Dieter Troutner would accompany me inside the chateau.

In front of the Chateau we slowly approached a huge solid oak door and I pushed the ringer bell. We heard no sound from inside so I pushed the plunger again and waited, still no response. Dieter tried the knob and turned it. The door was not locked and it slowly opened exposing the interior of a magnificent vestibule, beyond which lay an expansive great room. It was furnished in Napoleonic period and we stared at the opulence in awe. Finally, I said, "Sergeant, go upstairs and see what's around. I'll check down here." Dieter responded, "Yes, Sir," and left with his M-1 at the ready. As he disappeared up the staircase, I became fascinated at what I saw.

The great room was certainly designed for comfort and relaxation. On one side was a huge fireplace and on the opposite wall large windows looked out over a small lake surrounded by tall spruce trees and flower beds which unfortunately at this time of the year lay dormant. It was obvious tender loving care had not been absent from this place for long.

Beside the large windows were seven foot high bookcases filled with leather bound books. Plush leather chairs and sofas surrounded richly finished solid oak tables and a magnificent candelabra with fresh candles in it hung from the center of the ceiling. On a serving table beneath the windows were several bottles of good German liquors: *Jagermeister* and *Asbach Urault.*

Prominently displayed nearby on a period grand piano was a photograph of a German officer, an Oberst (Colonel). No one was around so I decided to help myself to a small offering of the *Asbach Urault.* I had learned to like it during my trips via my 2000 timeline to Germany. As I stood among all this beauty and history sipping to my delight, I picked up the photo....

When suddenly, a noise penetrated the stillness. There was someone behind me. Startled by the unknown, I dropped the photo and heard the glass shatter and tinkle as it struck the floor. I grabbed my M-1, abruptly turned and was taken aback; standing erect and silently in the doorway was a very attractive yet serious appearing woman of about 35 years.

We both stood transfixed as if our feet were planted in concrete, looking directly into each others eyes. She certainly had my attention, but my thoughts were confused. Pointing my rifle away from her I tried to smile, but her eyes had shifted to the broken photo on the floor. I sensed the photograph was important to her; thus, picked it up, took a few steps toward her, handed it to her, stuttering, "I'm sorry, Mam."

She took the photograph, sadly looked at it and tears filled her eyes. I sensed, perhaps this was her husband

and asked her in German if it was. After a short time she replied, "*Ja, das war mein Mann und er ist tot.* (Yes, that was my husband and he is dead). *Mein name ist* (My name is) Madame Janette Marie von Kluge." I assumed she and Herr Oberst had somehow inherited the chateau after the fall of France in 1940; however, that was an assumption not worth pursuing at this time.

I continued, "Madame von Kluge, I am Lieutenant Fred Mitchell, Third US Army at your pleasure, Mam." I had by this time settled down and would now describe Madame von Kluge as 5'4", slim, wavy dark brown hair, beautiful penetrating brown eyes, what anyone would call one very impressive lady.

Staff Sergeant Troutner having heard the commotion hurried down the stairs, and as soon as he saw Madame von Kluge, he stopped and stood rigidly erect. I introduced him to Madame von Kluge, and in a manner dictated by his rank, Sergeant Troutner immediately snapped to attention, clicked his heels, removed his helmet, tucked it under his left arm, and in a delightful southern accent said, "At your pleasure, Mam."

Frankly I wasn't sure what my next action should be when to my relief Madame von Kluge smiled and in English said, "How gallant you gentlemen are. You are the first American soldiers I have had the pleasure of meeting. Please, Lieutenant, continue your drink and offer your Sergeant one too." Dieter said, "We thank you, Mam," and quickly poured himself a hefty slug. We both raised our glasses in unison.

I asked if there was anything we could do for her? Was she in need of food or anything? She smiled politely and replied that she had everything she required. We finished our drinks, told her we were sorry to have bothered her, and accordingly we would leave. She smiled and replied, "Again, Gentlemen, my thanks.... and Lieutenant Mitchell, *I have a feeling we shall meet again."* I answered, "Yes, Madame, and that would be my pleasure."

We then left via the front door. On our way back to our jeeps Dieter asked, “Sir, what the deuce did that we’ll meet again mean?” I grinned at him, said, “Sergeant, it beats the hell out of me. Gotta admit though, wouldn’t mind it at all.”

We both chuckled and upon reaching our jeeps I waved my arms above my head and shouted for the pickets to rejoin the column. When they were accounted for said, “Okay, let’s head this outfit north a piece, and at our first chance we’ll move west and see what lays out thata way.”

For the rest of the morning we slowly crept our way north, stopping occasionally to observe the country ahead and to both sides of us. We uneventfully had covered a distance of about four miles. Surprisingly the countryside seemed peaceful and quiet. We passed a lot of cows grazing harmlessly in solitude as though their world was entirely at peace, yet, I noted the cattle appeared to be well fed and recently milked. Sorta like life was normal around here. After stopping for a brief lunch and a cigarette I radioed my first report of the day, without noting our stop at the chateau, "Recon 1, so far all quiet… over and out."

I sent one jeep on ahead to find a road, path, or something where we could move our small column west. We had been provided with reports that suggested Germans were in the vicinity, but so far no sightings of them. Shortly, Corporal Crawford radioed me that about three miles north he had located a narrow road heading west through what looked like a heavily wooded area, but it appeared passable. I replied, "Good show, Corporal, we'll be right up." The rest of us climbed aboard our jeeps and scurried north.

When we arrived I surveyed the area with my binoculars and everything remained serene which greatly concerned me. Air recon had documented enemy forces nearby but their exact whereabouts and strength were unknown; however, they were undoubtedly on the move.

I guessed we had better locate them; thus, we turned west and soon the road narrowed to a point where a tank could barely traverse it single file. I told my drivers to turn their jeeps around and continue by backing up in case we needed to make a rapid retreat and exit the woods quickly; we would then be headed in the right direction.

From this point we would proceed on foot. I left three drivers with the jeeps, Crawford, Hepburn, and Kelly. Private First Class Caesar would proceed ahead as our point. The rest of us followed the road in staggered file.

After awhile in the distance to our front we could hear commotion, faintly at first but increasing. Suddenly Private First Class Caesar, our point man, appeared from around a curve running as fast as he could toward us. Out of breath he hastened to me, saluted, said, "Sir, Panzers! Sounds like several of them, couldn't see any troops, but they must be near!" I agreed and told Sergeant Marcello and Private Bell that they should come with me and told my remaining group should they encounter overwhelming force to mount up and get the hell out of here. However, if only enemy scouts appeared then remain as a blocking force.

Then Sergeant Marcello, Private Bell and I left on foot and headed toward the commotion to more precisely determine what was happening. Meantime Private First Class Ford radioed headquarters we had sighted an enemy force of unknown strength and were continuing to scout it.

Before long we encountered the German patrol and immediately took cover in a shallow ditch where I told Marcello and Bell to take careful aim and open fire. As I fired my M-1, I experienced very mixed emotions. *My future recollections of this day will conflict with my present feelings of what I now must do. It seems I am today going to fire on future friends, who today just happen to be my enemies. Of course, I must do whatever is required to protect my men and live with whatever the consequences of my actions may be. Right now I feel as though I am on a giant wave being swept along by this ocean of time.*

Abruptly a bullet, reminding me of a bee in flight, whizzed past my ear and thudded dramatically into the tree next to my head. That shocked me back to today's reality. Now everyone was firing as fast as they could pull their triggers, ammo clips zinged from our rifles, and we quickly reloaded.

Unexpectedly a German soldier with his weapon raised was running straight toward me and without thought I squeezed my trigger and in a flash my M-1 fired. The enemy soldier grabbed his chest, his knees crumpled, and his rifle flew from his grip. As he fell his frightened eyes were wide open looking right at me, his mouth was agape as if to say, *Why did you do this*? He fell to both knees, then face forward onto the ice cold turf of immortality.

As I stand here in the freezing snow viewing the sight of a person whom I have just killed, I pondered, how can I live with what I have just done? Yet in this place of horror and destruction, as a young man, I am living in a time when this is my honorable duty. Therefore, I suppose in some ironic way, I should be honored for my opportunity to experience what this generation of young Americans are offering up in order to insure the future of our way of life. In this way I shall always be proud to have contributed to those future years of well being. God bless America.

Fortunately my adrenaline flow had awakened me back to reality. I waved my arms toward the rear and hollered, "Let's get the shit out of here," and we took off running, ducking, and dodging behind trees until we reached a reasonable distance of safety. We stopped for a moment to catch our breath and to reload our rifles before continuing our withdrawal to locate the remainder of Recon 1.

When we reached our jeeps, I grabbed the radio and reported we had made contact with German panzers and infantry. I said, "Cannot determine their numbers, but there are several of them, and they are probably accompanied by infantry of at least battalion strength. We've done as much as we can here and request instructions." We were ordered to maneuver our way back to base and keep our eyes open. I answered, "Yes, Sir, over and out." I ordered, " Okay, you guys, remount, we're moving back."

Next we heard the familiar rolling, whirring, swooshing sound overhead of our inbound artillery rounds. They exploded on the ground blanketing with shrapnel the area from which we had only a very few moments ago vacated. We all just shuddered and thought, *better them than us.*

However, I couldn't get out of my mind the sight of that young German soldier falling to the ground, looking at me as though my killing him was something personal. I am certain his image will haunt me forever, and am learning again what goes with being a soldier involved in mortal combat with the enemy.

The artillery shelling continued for the next ten minutes, when suddenly at least a dozen Army Air Corps P-47 Thunderbolts, their tails painted a brilliant red, screamed by and continued the pasting job the artillery had started. I felt sorrow for those poor German bastards who were on the receiving end of what must be devastating horror, but reasoned, *wasn't me who started this God damn war, so file your complaints with Herr Hitler.*

It took us over two hours to wander back to headquarters where Captain Horne was awaiting my report. By now it was beginning to get dark and we were very hungry. Captain Horne instructed my men to proceed to the mess hall, told me to have a seat and he would order in a couple meals. As we dined I briefed him on what Recon 1 had learned which was little, except it appeared to me as though the Germans got a real pasting as they were moving to the north. Additionally, we had seen many trucks laden, I supposed, with supplies. His eyes seemed to light up as he said, "Thank you, Lieutenant. Good that you gave them trouble, and your sighting of trucks and panzers moving northward could bare some significance."

* * * * *

Captain Horne said, "Recon 1 will stand down until 3 December; therefore, report to me here for orders, details of your area, and your objectives at 0730 on 1 December. Have Recon 1 ready and equipped with at least five days rations. This may be a big one for you."

I could tell from his tone something was mounting, but until 1 December we had a few days to relax and prepare. Sergeants Troutner, Marcello, and myself went over everything, the jeeps, the radio, petrol, and food supplies. I spent time with Corporal Temple (Medic) and Private First Class Ford (Radioman) to insure everything was ready with them, especially Corporal Temple. He would need more than his usual supplies of medicines. I knew what it was that we were heading for; we had to have all bases covered.

Between preparations we ate, had a few beers at the canteen, and took in whatever entertainment was available. The time passed quickly. At 0730 on 1

December, Sergeants Troutner, Marcello and myself met as ordered with Captain Horne and Intelligence Officer, Major Larson, who detailed our patrol area and objectives. They were:

1. Leave at 0530 on 3 December and retrace the route of our last patrol of 26 November.
2. Assess the makeup of and damage inflicted on the German force which was attacked there on the 26th.
3. By radio, report whatever you find, and keep your reports brief but frequent.
4. Continue northwest toward Boulay (about 15 miles).
5. Interrogate locals whenever possible. Any trace of information on German activities may well be important.
6. If you are detected by enemy forces, do not offer a fire fight. Retire by any route available.
7. Return here as your situation dictates.

During 2 December all members of Recon 1 underwent a briefing by me on how I viewed our upcoming patrol. We would be on a seek-out information patrol, and ordered to avoid firefights. Only myself or Sergeants Troutner and Marcello should attempt interrogation of any locals we might encounter.

At 0530 on 3 December our intrepid patrol of three jeeps and eleven men ventured out from American lines. There were no bands, no cheers or hurrahs, only the sound of silence accompanied us as we departed our base. The only noticeable presences were a dark, starless, cold morning, and a light snow whipping across our front. A great day for Eskimos, polar bears, and reconnaissance patrols!

It took us three hours to reach the point where we had encountered the German patrol on 26 November. We proceeded slowly as we approached the area where the artillery and Air Force had hit the German columns heading north. We counted 21 supply vehicles of various types, six artillery pieces, and 5 panzers destroyed. All else had either escaped or had been hauled off by the Germans. Not as much damage as I had expected. There were no civilian farms nearby; thus, no one was around who could be interrogated.

I reported my initial findings to headquarters at 0930. Then our patrol mounted up and we began our slow journey toward Boulay. It was getting colder and the snow, now a wee bit heavier, was blowing directly in our faces from the north. The morning temperature had reached only 28F and our breath formed pretty little white cloud formations. It was a picturesque, eerily silent, yet miserable day. For sure the Germans were now some miles distant to our north and probably still nestled down this morning in their tents and blankets.

We managed the remaining 10 miles, arriving at the outskirts of Boulay at 1100 hours. Boulay was a farming community of maybe 3,000 people built around important connecting roads arriving from all directions.

As no Germans were in sight our small patrol slowly entered the town and was soon surrounded by joyous civilians, many armed with wine, throwing kisses, and waving French flags. None of us spoke French and had to rely on our German.

Finally Monsieur Francois Cotier, who spoke German, arrived. He said he was the Mayor, welcomed us to Boulay, and planted a kiss on my cheek. I said, "Thank you, Mayor, but we are not occupying the town, only trying to locate the Germans. Have you seen any lately?"

I guess he understood me and said, "*Ja, Ja, mein fruend*! Hundreds, maybe thousands of them, all aboard dozens and dozens of lories passed through Boulay on the road northwest toward Saarlouis. I counted 53 panzers, there may have been more, and a hundred or more artillery pieces with caissons." He thought it unusual so many soldiers and so much equipment were headed in that direction, and so did I. I thanked the mayor graciously and headed for the radio.

When I reached Major Larson, I reported… "Got something here, Sir, am scrambling it." He acknowledged, "Roger, Recon 1, go ahead." I reported we had reached Boulay with no enemy contact and the Mayor had described a large column of panzers, artillery and trucks with mounted infantry headed northwest toward Saarlouis. Instructions please, over." Major Larson, said "Good report, Lieutenant. If possible maintain Recon 1 near Boulay on the possibility more Germans will be passing through there. Your report may indicate a buildup by the Germans is underway to the north of you." I replied, "Yes, Sir, it does seem that way, Willco, over and out."

I told Mayor Cotier we had been ordered to return to our base, wished him well, waved at the crowd and said, "Hopefully, we shall return." Our little column chugged out of town in an apparent hurry, but we weren't retreating. About a mile east from Boulay there was a dense wooded area from where we could observe all roads in and out of the village. It was a relatively protected area, somewhat out of the wind, and we pitched our pup tents. We could not build a fire; thus, it was going to be a cold night with cold food.

We stood two hour watches of two men at a time. Since there were eleven of us, I would be odd man out. But not really, for every hour I would be making a check. The temperature dropped to 22F, exceptionally cold for early December but generally our great coats, pup tents, and blankets kept us fairly comfortable. It was the absence of hot coffee and hot food that really hurt.

Morning broke early at 0500. Throughout the night we continued to hear the sounds of heavy traffic. Panzers and troops were definitely on the move north. We had to stay quietly hunkered down as the Germans certainly would have patrols out on their flanks; therefore, we could only guess at what was going on. I reported to headquarters what we had heard from our observation point and it appeared the Germans were reoccupying Boulay. Major Larson accepted my report and reasoned Recon 1's position was becoming tenuous; thus, he ordered us to return to base.

Our mission had accomplished as much as it could so I simply said, "Yes, Sir, Willco, over and out." We loaded up our jeeps and happily high tailed it toward American lines. So far we had been fortunate to not have incurred casualties, and hoped our good luck would continue. Our patrol had certainly been shorter than we anticipated.

After debriefing, Captain Horne advised me that, subject to change, "Recon 1's next patrol is scheduled for 7 December, and once again it will probably be an extended sojourn. Until then, make certain your vehicles are up to snuff, and relax."

It seemed very unusual we would have this much time between patrols, but I sure wasn't going to complain. Everyone got a two day pass to visit a rest and recreation area located about 10 miles west of Metz. Movies, canteens, soft clean beds, hot showers, and the USO which hopefully meant movie stars and pretty girls serving doughnuts; of course, all look no touch. But no matter, to us it was heaven on earth for two whole days.

* * * * *

While my squad left for their outing, I borrowed a jeep from headquarters and drove to the village of Lemont where my father, Mathew, was buried in the town's church graveyard. This was my second visit, *having been here with Shirley in 1969.* It took me a little over an hour and as I entered Lemont I was surprised at its appearance. In every way it was an area which obviously had changed very little for many, many years. Untouched by war it was a serene place and I felt certain my father would have loved it.

For the first time in the last several days the sun was shining and a gentle warm wind was wafting across the cemetery. As I had been here before, I proceeded to dad's site, a simple granite marker which bore the inscription:

First Lieutenant
Mathew Dale Mitchell
26 Squadron, United States
Air Corps, 8 June, 1918

I stood respectively at attention at the foot of my father's grave. My emotions were on full speed, much more so than during my first visit; I suppose because it was wartime. I never knew my dad, but standing here, 26 years after his death, in the army, in France, at war with the Germans, somehow it had a very surreal meaning to me like, *and we are doing it all over again*. I could not help myself, as tears swelled up in my eyes.

There was a little bench nearby; so, I eventually sat down and reflected on how dad's last day might have occurred. *I tried to put myself in his place, in his cockpit. What were his last thoughts?* I had read the army's report, including his wingman's statement and was satisfied dad never suffered. *I hoped it was like the lights just went out, and then there was only serenity, only peace.*

It was so pleasant here; I wanted to stay longer, but I couldn't. After a time, I got up, walked to dad's marker, and just stood, erect, and at last said out loud, "*Dad, I love you, I always have. It seems to me we have always been friends and always shall be. You know that mom will always love you too. But I have to go now, dad, and help win our war in hope somehow, this time, it might make this a better world. Hope springs eternal, doesn't it, dad?*"

Continuing to stand quietly, there was a gentle tap on my left shoulder. I turned and almost fainted. There standing face-to-face with me was *my father* attired in his WWI flying suit. I recognized him immediately from the many photos my mother had shown me. I remained frozen at attention, thinking, *Is this a dream?*

He appeared so real as he said, gently, "Son, those were fine words you just said. Thank you, couldn't have asked for anything more. We have only a little time so I'll be brief. I am so very proud of you, Fred, and wish we could have gotten to know each other. You are the epitome of everything I could hope you would be. But remember,

I did, and you are doing, that which we know is best for our families and our country. So go with God and honor, armed with the righteousness of your cause." *I remained stupefied, frozen. I couldn't speak.*

Then dad took my hand, shook it, saluted, and walked slowly away until he just faded into the scenery, back to his eternal rest. As he departed I saluted, stood silently for a moment, did an about face, returned to my jeep, and slowly left. I was now crying unabashedly, and did so for most of my drive back to camp and to the reality of my war.... My lasting memory of this meeting with my father was that when he shook my hand...*his hands were warm?*

Upon my return to camp, I immediately started checking Recon 1's readiness for our sojourn back into the unpleasantness of another cold and snowy mission. It had begun to snow. I was not surprised.

* * * * *

On the Afternoon of 6 December Sergeants Troutner, Marcello, and myself reported to Major Larson's headquarters. Captain Horne was also in attendance. We seated ourselves in front of a large map mounted on the wall. After greeting us and having coffee served Major Larson took a pointer in hand and said, "Men, I have a tough job for you and Recon 1. Notice that our front line runs somewhat parallel to the roads leading from Metz to Thionville which is about 25 miles to our north. Right now we control approximately the first five miles and from there the rest is literally a hodgepodge. Sometimes the road is within our lines, sometimes it is in no-man's-land, and sometimes it is within German lines.

"It is imperative we know the strength the Germans have in those areas which are not controlled by American forces. And that, Gentlemen, will be a dangerous undertaking. Are there any questions or comments?"

After a few minutes consulting the map I said, "Sir's, I do have a few comments." Major Larson replied, "Of course, Lieutenant, please proceed." I continued, "It seems to me we will be hard pressed to avoid a fire fight or two. Therefore, I'd like to retrofit Recon 1 with a little heavy artillery. Namely create a couple, two man b.a.r. (browning automatic rifle) teams, and secondly we carry rifle grenade ammo to substitute for the lack of any mortar support."

Captain Horne spoke up, "Sir, I concur with Lieutenant Mitchell's recommendations. Private First Class Caesar and Corporal Crawford are qualified b.a.r. men." Major Larson replied, "Good, if you can get the changes made in time, go to it. Recon 1 will depart 0730 in the morning from our advance position on the road to Thionville." I answered, "Yes, Sir, and thank you, we'll be ready in time."

* * * * *

Immediately I ordered Sergeant Troutner to assemble our squad for a briefing. When everyone was present, I began, "Men, we have got a good one here, and we have lots to do before we leave on our little vacation in the morning at 0730.

"Sergeant Troutner you will be in charge of equipping and organizing the two b.a.r. and the two rifle grenade teams. Corporal Temple make sure you take along additional medical supplies, this one could get real mean in a hurry. On this sojourn we have no orders to avoid a fight. Sergeant Marcello, requisition double rations for seven days and strap as many extra gasoline jerry cans as possible onto each jeep. Any questions?" There were none; thus, I told the guys to get humping as there was a hell of a lot of work to be done.

We were awakened at 0500. Awakened was an extraneous word for I doubted any of us slept much, if any. At 0730 we were assembled. I gave Recon 1 a once-over and said,

"OK, Gentlemen, start your engines and let's get this show on the road." Staff Sergeant Troutner, Corporal Crawford, Private First Class Caesar, and Private Bell were on the lead jeep, followed by me, Private First Class Ford (radioman), and Private Purdy. Bringing up the rear was Sergeant Marcello, Private Kelly, Private Hepburn, and Medic, Corporal Temple.

At precisely 0754 in the distance we could faintly hear a bugle sounding taps. It had been ordered by General Patton to be blown at all headquarter locations of the Third Army in memory of the Japanese attack at 0754 at Pearl Harbor on December 7,1941.

For a moment the haunting strains caused my memory to warp back to that date. *For I, then Commander Fred D. Mitchell, was there on that date along with Lieutenant Commander John Paul Kincaid, Lieutenant Junior Grade, Carole Foster, and Ensign Thomas Coerper.* All were US Naval personnel. God, I miss them so much.... But today, I now have another command to concern myself with.

On the road from Metz to Bastogne it seemed everyday was a carbon copy, cold, blustery, and with light to moderate snow falling. It gave a false impression that everything was clean, beautiful and at peace, even though we could hear the distant rumbling of warfare. My mind wondered, *Yeh, a lovely day for a quiet little drive through a pristine French countryside.*

We were still well within American lines and our first 4 miles were easy, but as we closed on Moselles we had to detour west for about a mile as the town was occupied by a German blocking force of unknown size. Earlier I had been informed that an American attack from the west of Moselles would take place this morning, an effort designed to free the town and force the Germans eastward. Hopefully, the resulting commotion would provide Recon 1 with cover enabling us to continue our movement north.

Thus, we waited until the attack began, an infantry assault accompanied by several Sherman tanks. During the noise, smoke, and confusion our three jeeps used this opportunity to head north for a couple of miles and then via a small farming path cross country intersecting again with the main road where we resumed our northern direction.

So far, so good, and that left us with about 18 or 19 miles to Moselles. For some reason, I felt very uneasy about this patrol and hoped our good luck would not run out, but I feared it would. Thinking under my breath, *Bob, old partner, keep a watchful eye on us; I feel like a poor little lamb who has lost his way and may need your help.* Well, anyway it was a good thought but whatever happens Bob will not intervene. Though believing I would survive this venture, I feared for my men. My stomach was churning.

Fortunately the land ahead was open and relatively flat; we couldn't see anything resembling Germans. That is until someone in our point jeep, which was about a 100 yards to our front, began frantically waving his arms. By the time we closed up we could see and hear what was of concern. Dust was rising in the distance and the distinct sound of tanks on the move got our attention. Panzers! They have a different sound from that of our Sherman tanks. I pondered, *Christ, now what, Fred? Do we cut and run? Do we try to hide and hope they will just pass us by? Or do we stand and fight?*

My analysis of the situation at hand was that our guys fighting to push the Germans out of Moselles might easily be overcome if we just let this German relief column go by us unchecked. *Therefore we will stand, fight, and try for an ambush of our own.* I informed my band of brothers this was as far as we are going to go without a fight. We have chosen an iffy situation, but it's now, or run away with our tails dragging. Everyone said, "Let's have at it, Lieutenant, we came here to win a war, vacation time is definitely now over."

A thicket of trees and a stone fence about 50 yards from the road seemed an appropriate place for our stand. We sat up our two b.a.r. teams about 30 yards apart amid some tall grass, and hunkered down in a shallow ditch behind the fence. I placed two men with rifle grenades at the edge of the wooded area and the rest of us, Corporal Temple, Private First Class Ford, myself, Privates Kelly and Hepburn would provide as much cover fire as we could. *I looked around and just for a moment I felt a little like what Lieutenant Colonel George Armstrong Custer must have felt at the Battle of the Little Big Horn back in 1874.*

My final command was, “Wait until I fire and then create as much hell as you can. You rifle grenadiers, I don’t expect you to hit much, but pump those grenades in there and hope that for awhile they’ll think we have mortars.”

Next I radioed headquarters, gave them our approximate location and said, “We have unknown numbers of panzers and infantry moving south toward Moselles. We’ll stop ’em for a little while, but get some air or artillery in here if you can. I don’t think we can hold them without it for long.”

Headquarters response was not too comforting. "Air is temporarily grounded by weather and most of our artillery is beyond your range. There is one battery just barely within range; we'll see if they can send you some rounds." I replied, "Aye, Aye, Skipper." *For a moment my military language had hearkened me back to my time at Pearl Harbor in 1941, but guess it didn't matter.*

Covered with mounted infantry, the first panzers were advancing across our front. I gave the command, *fire!* The five of us including medic Temple began blasting away at the two lead tanks. Simultaneously the chat, chat, chat of our automatic rifles resounded and we could hear the rounds pinging as they struck the panzers. German soldiers who were mounted on them began falling like wet sandbags. Then our rifle grenades began dropping among the walking infantry as fast as Bell and Purdy could load and fire.

Suddenly, it seemed, Germans were collapsing all over the place, from the tanks where they were riding and from within their marching ranks as well. Our aim was good and initially confusion in their ranks was evident.

But I knew surprise was only temporary and soon panzers would be blowing our positions from here to eternity. We continued firing for about four minutes; then, I ordered our little band to mount our jeeps and head east as fast as we could until it was safe to turn south and head back toward American lines. I was pleased we had temporarily halted the Germans. It would take them time to reorganize and continue their advance. I radioed headquarters informing them of such.

As we boarded our jeeps several 105mm artillery rounds noisily tumbled overhead. Everyone shouted, "Incoming, incoming, that'll hold 'em in place for awhile." The resulting explosions were music to our ears. We departed the area and stopped to take count. Sergeant Wayne Marcello had a gaping wound in his side and Corporal Temple was administering morphine and was working feverishly to get the bleeding under control.

Suddenly, as I took headcount, Corporal Ben Crawford along with his b.a.r. was missing. No one could account for what happened to him and that struck home hard. There is no worse feeling than to loose a comrade, let alone not know what happened to him. But we could not go back, only pray that Corporal Crawford was wounded or captured.

It was time to get the hell out of here while we still could. In total things had gone well and I was pleased at Recon 1's actions; hoped headquarters would see it that way too.

Back at headquarters, Staff Sergeant Troutner and I reported to Major Larson and Captain Horn. We advised them of our loss of Corporal Crawford; they expressed regret, but hurriedly returned to the results of today's patrol.

Moselles had been retaken. At least in part as a result of Recon 1's actions. A force of Third Army tanks and infantry had been given time to be redirected, and they intercepted the arriving Germans, whose force they either destroyed, took prisoner, or forced to retreat. Moselles had been saved, and Major Larson said, "Lieutenant, your group gets a lot of the credit."

I replied, "Thank you, Sir, and as a result of our losses will you please have orders cut for promotions: Private First Class Frank Caesar to Corporal and Private Burt Hepburn to Private First Class? Also, Sir, I will need a replacement for Corporal Crawford."

Major Larson nodded his head, "Consider the promotions done, and I'll find a good replacement for you, hopefully by tomorrow." I snapped a salute, said, "Thank you, Sir," did an about face, and returned to my tired, dirty, and hungry squad. 7 December had been a fateful day. I informed my group that in the words of headquarters, we were given much of the credit for saving the day at Moselles. Until we heard something to the contrary we had a post pass, with instructions to not leave the area. That meant hot showers, hot meals, movies, doughnuts, coffee, and hopefully a few beers and some pretty USO girls to look at.

* * * * *

The following morning Corporal Chris Wilson, Crawford's replacement, reported for duty and hurriedly I introduced him to the men of Recon 1. Chris was a welcome addition to my little outfit. He had been with Patton since Normandy, spoke some German, and seemed an all around take-no-shit guy. Our outfit was now back up to strength and we spent the following days reviewing our routines… *As a traveler in time I had studied and knew broadly what lay in front of us. Not in detail, but as history had laid it out.*

* * * * *

Our respite had lasted for over a week but it ended at 1300 on 16 December when I was summoned to

Captain Horne's headquarters. *I knew at once, it was Bastogne.*

At dawn on the morning of 16 December, during one of the coldest winters in history, the Germans launched a major offensive through the Ardennes Forest in southern Belgium. Amassing 29 Divisions totaling 250,000 men in an area weakly defended by the Americans, the Germans intended first to cross the Meuse River and then reach Brussels, thus, splitting allied forces and throwing them back to the English Channel. The sea would give German's the advantage. Allied forces could be destroyed piecemeal by German panzer divisions and the Luftwaffe.

The offensive would nominally be under the command of Field Marshal Gird von Rundstedt, but the main thrust of the Ardennes Offensive would be provided by General Hasso Eccard von Manteuffel's Fifth Panzer Army. Manteuffel was a brilliant panzer tactician earning his reputation in Russia during 1942-44; thus, he was used to fighting a winter war.

When Staff Sergeant Troutner and I arrived at Captain Horne's command tent he anxiously said, "Come in and sit down." On our way we noticed everyone excitedly scurrying from here-to-there and everywhere in between. Sergeant Troutner said, "Lieutenant, what's going on?" Although I actually knew, my reply was a distant, "Sergeant, beats the hell out of me, guess we'll find out soon enough." As we entered the command tent, mounted on an easel in front of us was a large map showing the countryside to our north from Metz to several miles beyond Luxemburg City. Captain Horne began, "Lieutenant, Sergeant, we got a huge job on our hands and Recon 1 has got a chunk of it to chew on."

Although the temperature in the tent was probably around 35F Captain Larson was sweating profusely, his eyes were almost glassy, and he stuttered a bit as he gestured rather uncontrollably with his hand toward the large map. I had never seen these traits in our captain before; thus, we imagined what was coming was something drastic. To our relief, as Captain Larson continued to speak, he relaxed and his demeanor began to return to normal.

Pointing to his map he began, "Gentlemen, here's your assignment. In massive strength the Germans have overrun American positions in the Ardennes Forest north of Luxemburg City. General Patton has ordered sizeable units of Third Army to rotate 90 degrees from their westward movements to due north and move rapidly as possible to the relief of the breakthrough, some 90 miles distant.

"Obviously this effort will be of superhuman proportions, and we will need eyes on the ground along the way. This, Lieutenant, along with other recon units will be your challenge. Recon 1's work has been very successful so far. Let us hope it continues."

I thought, *OK, knew the German blitzkrieg in the Ardennes was coming, and the warm ups are now over.* After a brief time to reflect on what had just been told us, I looked at Captain Larson and said, "Yes, Sir,

Captain, Recon 1 will do it, Sir. May we spend some time looking over your maps before we go?" He replied, "Of course, Lieutenant, and ask questions if you have them." I nodded and Troutner and I approached the command map.

After about 15 minutes of discussion and reviewing things on the map with Staff Sergeant Troutner, I asked, "Sir, in what position will you want us in respect to Third Army's lead units, and when do you want us moving?" Captain Larson replied, "Lieutenant, Third Army will be moving north by 0500 in the morning, 17 December. Recon 1 must be out by no later than 0400, and you will assume your location as point on the north and somewhat west of Third Army's movement. Is that clear?"

So point it was to be. OK, I looked at Captain Larson, replied, "Sir, that is very clear. We'll leave now and be on point by 0400 in the morning. We are already supplied and ready. We thank you, Sir," saluted, turned and left the command tent.

As we walked back to our squad area, I looked at Troutner, slapped my helmet and said, "For Christ sake, Sergeant, looks like we're going to have a snoot full of trouble on this excursion." He answered, "Beggen your pardon, Sir, but I think that could be the understatement of the year." I responded, "Yeh, Sergeant, you are probably right." When we reached our bivouac area, I asked Sergeant Troutner to assemble the men in my squad tent as soon as possible for a briefing on tomorrow's mission. I knew they'd be *pleased as hell* about this one.

It was now 1400 on 16 December. I thought, *Only 8 more days until Christmas and my mind raced back to my other Christmases at home with my family and friends. Often there was snow falling, just like it is here, and we were listening to Christmas carols on the radio.*

Then as my men began to arrive, reality raced right back. I told them to sit wherever they could, on my bed, at my makeshift desk, on my foot locker, or on the wooden floor. Their mood was somber as they expected me to lay out some grueling mission; I would not disappoint them.

I began, "OK, Recon 1, here we go. At 0400 tomorrow morning we will assume the point for a move of Third Army. Massive German forces have broken through our lines about 90 miles north of here, and General Patton is moving to intercept the breakthrough. It will be a tough trip and we will be the lead boots on the ground, the eyes for General Patton.

"We are loaded and ready, so we will push off at 0400, breakfast at 0300. I suggest that you all write a quick letter to your loved ones for it'll be some time before you will have another chance. To all of us good fortune; see you at breakfast. Dismissed."

I had asked for questions, that I was certain my men might have, but they never asked any and that was good as I had no answers. Slowly in ones and twos everyone except Staff Sergeant Troutner left my tent. When we were alone, I said, "Dieter, my trusted friend, this is going to be hell and test all our tenacities. At all times, Sergeant, hold tight, keep the men alert, and have faith in what we are doing. Now get out of here and get some rest." Dieter, smiled, saluted, said goodnight, turned and left.

Like a bolt from the blue I felt very alone on this, what would probably be my last quiet night in 1944 France. I then prepared myself for bed, certain this would be a restless night. It was warm inside my sleeping bag and for some reason unknown to me, I was soon nominally asleep.

The next thing I was totally aware of was when the duty orderly awakened me. It was 0230, time to hurriedly get into my winter clothing, and rush to what would likely be my last hot meal for quite some time. After breakfast those who wrote letters home verily had time to mail them.

No more second guessing now, it was 0400 and time to move out. As we boarded our three jeeps I reflected,

This is what I have been waiting for. Bastogne here we come. The year 2000 seemed a millennium away. Is it possible that it may be plodding along right beside me?

Our jeep's engines roared, officially announcing the start of our quest, and my mind once again zinged back to reality. I turned to my driver, Private First Class Burt Hepburn, patted him on the helmet, said, "OK, soldier, you have a long tough road to go, so get us there." He looked at me, "Don't know where there is, Sir, but wherever it is, I'll get us there." He smiled, as he tossed me a mini salute. I acknowledged, "Fine, Burt, I know you will, but for the duration of this trip no more saluting, just keep your eyes on the road."

We were on our way and in about 15 minutes we arrived at our front lines; everything was uncommonly still. As we crossed into no-man's-land I raised my right arm, clinched my fist, and motioned us forward. Our first objective was to reconnoiter the road and surrounding territory between the American front lines and Thionville, a medium sized city located at a major crossroads about 25 miles to our north. How long it will take will depend on enemy activity. We covered the first five miles in one hour. That was good considering we were in enemy territory, and it allowed us time to send out lateral patrols. We stayed in radio contact with our headquarters at all times; thus, Patton's lead columns were made aware of any *Wehrmacht* (army) activity we spotted or encountered.

It seemed to me a considerable amount of time had passed until we approached the outskirts of Thionville, yet so far there had been no signs of enemy activity. I told Sergeant Wilson to take Privates Bell and Purdy in a jeep and enter the town. We had to know if it was occupied, and if it was, we needed to call for support and have the town cleared of enemy forces before Patton's columns arrived.

Sergeant Wilson's jeep crept slowly past the first buildings with weapons at ready. Everything was strangely silent and as they proceeded he did not see evidence of any enemy presence. After traveling for several blocks Wilson radioed back that all was quiet. Evidently Thionville was clear of German forces, which seemed a bit strange to me.

Yet, I motioned my patrol ahead and as we entered the town we began to see flags appearing in some of the windows, French, American, Belgian, and a few white. People were starting to come out into the street, some clapping and waving, and some shouting, "*Americain, Americain.*"

Obviously the Germans were gone, probably concentrating their efforts further to the north. We notified Third Army that Thionville was secure. It was now late morning and we did not expect leading elements of Third Army to arrive until late afternoon, so Recon 1 would camp in Thionville tonight and begin patrolling north at 0500 from there on 18 December. Our objective would be to cautiously proceed north toward Luxembourg City still some 25 miles distant until we encounter German activity.

In the morning our little band proceeded north from Thionville to a point approximately three miles beyond the village of Hettange where we encountered a motorized *Wehrmacht* patrol who had spotted us at the same time. We observed a couple of armored cars and obviously we couldn't move past them without help; thus, we asked for an air strike and suggested Third Army beef up our fire power by assigning us a couple Sherman tanks along with a squad of infantry. It would definitely be tougher from here on and we were obviously going to encounter enemy resistance beyond our available capabilities. There was still 25 miles before we would reach Luxembourg City.

Headquarters was quick to agree with my request and within fifteen minutes Thunderbirds from the Air Corps arrived, strafing and firing rockets into the German's midst. It didn't take them long before the armored vehicles were ablaze and the Germans were in retreat. When our tanks and infantry support arrived our reinforced Recon 1 immediately left Hettange following the Germans north.

Our designated route would take us north about ten miles to an intersection where we would turn west four miles to the village of Bettembourg and remain there until the lead elements of Third Army arrived. I expected to average maybe 2 mph; thus, it would probably take us until mid afternoon to arrive at Bettembourg.

However our advance was not with out incident; without warning shots rang out and Private Anson Purdy in the trailing jeep slumped forward. Immediately the machine gunners from our two Sherman's cut loose. The sniper was located in an abandoned house and was quickly disposed of. Fortunately Purdy wasn't too badly wounded. The bullet had passed through his left forearm without hitting any bone, lots of blood, painful, and in need of some suturing. Corporal Temple did all he could.

We arrived at the intersection to Bettembourg and found it obstructed by trees which had been felled and now crisscrossed the intersection. Additionally, the roads were surrounded on all sides for a couple of miles by deep gorges making the roads impassable for tanks and men alike. As we approached we were again the recipient of heavy sniper fire as well as considerable mortar fire incoming from the direction of Bettembourg.

Not a pretty picture, we had to clear the intersection and do it quickly. I posted men with automatic rifles on each side of the crossroads, ordered the two tank commanders to have the tree trunks tied to the rear of their tanks, and pull them away from the intersection. The tanks machine gunners and our automatic rifles poured a heavy fuselage of fifty and thirty caliber fire at the snipers. At the same time the tanks 75mm guns lobbed a few rounds in the direction of the mortar fire which for the present quieted them.

Within twenty minutes the trees had been cleared and we once again were able to continue our advance west to Bettembourg, But we suffered more casualties. One of the tank machine gunners sustained a serious wound to the head and my driver Private First Class Hepburn was hit in the right chest by a small piece of shrapnel from the mortar fire. Corporal Temple now had his hands full. Fortunately after Corporal Temple removed the shrapnel and patched him up Hepburn would be all right, and he insisted on continuing as my driver. As for the tank gunner, he was unconscious and needed further medical help. Temple had done all that he could.

Good news for us, the Germans once more continued to withdraw and the remaining distance to Bettembourg was now clear for our little group, who continued to act larger than they were, to proceed. We arrived at Bettembourg at 1630. We were in luck, the village church was being used as a makeshift hospital. Several wounded German soldiers had been left under the care of the local doctor, Dr. Claus Desons, the local clergy, Father Pierre Piedmont, and their helper, *Janette Marie von Kluge*. I was thunderstruck! How was it possible

Madame von Kluge would be here? However, she was not yet aware of my presence!

I radioed headquarters, "We have arrived at Bettembourg and the town is clear of any active Germans. There is a makeshift hospital here with some number of German wounded under the care of a local doctor. We have brought our wounded tanker to the hospital and will offer whatever assistance we can. I plan to stay in place here until your advance units arrive. Are there any further orders?" The reply was short. "Roger, Recon 1, your message is clear, no further orders."

We were all dead tired and except for three sentries I ordered everyone else to stand down. Reveille would be at 0500. We estimated lead elements of Third Army would arrive here around mid afternoon on the 19th. Man, it was cold! Some hot coffee would be great, but no fires again this night.

* * * * *

Morning of 19 December arrived and it was very overcast. No air cover could be expected today. I told my men, "When not on duty relax and see what if any hot food exists here. And remember we are guests so pay or barter for anything you get. Tomorrow you can expect we'll be on the last leg of our journey to *Bastogne.*" A subtle groan emerged from my usually composed band of brothers. Obviously, advance publicity from Bastogne had not left them with a favorable opinion.

* * * * *

At 0645 I left Staff Sergeant Troutner in charge and proceeded to the hospital to check on our tank gunner who was wounded. At least that was my excuse. Really I was anxious to see Madame von Kluge. *Could this be what she had in mind when she told me we would meet again? How could she have known?*

When I entered the hospital she was attending one of the more seriously wounded German soldiers, a Hauptman (Captain) from the 401st Panzer Lehr Division. As she noticed me she brushed back her dark brown hair, stood erect, and faintly smiled. At best she appeared worn out, perhaps unable at first to even recognize me.

I approached her, held out my hand, and softly spoke, "*Janette.*" She immediately grasped my hand, wavered a bit and stuttered, "Lieutenant Mitchell, Fred, my God, is it you? I am so surprised and pleased to see you." She again staggered slightly, grabbed hold of a bed post, but wiping her brow managed, "Please forgive me for how I must look. There has been much work to do here, so little time, so little medicine."

I pulled her near me, smiled, and placed a gentle kiss on her forehead replying, "Janette, to me you will always look lovely; this ordeal has only served to bring out your true beauty. You look perfectly delightful." I then lifted her chin and we looked into each others eyes; it was an exhilarating feeling. Gently I kissed her as sincerely as I could and it was obvious she appreciated my gesture of attention and affection. It was as if I had found a long lost love…and perhaps I had.

I continued, "Third Army's advance units will be here by mid afternoon and they will have a medical team with them and be able to attend the more seriously of your wounded." She answered, "Oh, Lieutenant, that will be so good. The good doctor has performed miracles, but his resources are miniscule. Thank you." I answered, "Janette, from now on, please, I am Fred, let's get out of here."

She replied, "Yes, Fred, let's leave this place, and I think now I must now tell you something before you find it out elsewhere…. I am the daughter-in-law of Field Marshal Guenther von Kluge. My husband, Colonel von Kluge, who was killed in Russia, was his son"…. That stopped me cold. I always suspected she was someone of importance, but this hit a home run like a sledge hammer. A von Kluge, yes, but that von Kluge. Wow!

I knew Field Marshal von Kluge, one in a long line of German Generals and Field Marshals, had recently committed suicide over disagreements with Hitler's Ardennes Offensive as he believed, and correctly so, the transfer of troops and material from the eastern front would deplete the Wehrmacht's capability to defend the Reich from further devastating Russian onslaughts.

To continue my surprise Janette added, "Fred will you please take me with you when you depart?…. I hope you might release me to General von Manteuffel's 5th Panzer Army, should we come in contact with them. I wish only to return to my family home near Munich. You see, General Manteuffel is a good friend of the von Kluge family." *I was shell shocked!…von Manteuffel… whose home Shirley and I had visited several times between 1969 and 1977 during our 2000 timeline.*

It took a few moments for everything to assimilate, then suddenly like out-of-control I replied, "Yes, yes, of course, Madame von Kluge, Janette, you can come with us when Recon 1 leaves in the morning. Just do not tell anyone you are going, okay?" She looked at me, gave me a huge hug and a kiss, smiled, and said, "Oh, Fred, you are so gallant, a true *Ritter* (Knight). I love you." *Wasn't real sure how to take all that*, but it did impress me.

I told Janette to be at Recon 1's encampment by 0430 in the morning, and to wear clothing suitable for the current cold and wet weather. I then returned to our camp and spent the rest of the day in contemplation of what had just been agreed to.

Janette would ride in my jeep along with Private First Class Hepburn, who was now patched up and insisted on continuing as my driver, along with my radioman Corporal Chris Ford. With the exception of Sergeant Troutner, I'll tell my men only that the lady accompanying us is a very important person and to treat her with respect.

I told Staff Sergeant Troutner, who was with me last November when we "visited" Madame von Kluge at her Chateau in France, what I intended to do. I then explained who she was, the daughter-in-law of Field Marshal Guenther von Kluge. I instructed Dieter to "play dumb" and act as though he did not know her previously and that we are hopefully trying to deliver her to General von Manteuffel. Of course Dieter agreed, "Certainly, Lieutenant, *Ich verstehen* (I understand)."

I looked up to the heavens and thought, *Bob, Bob, help if you can, ole Fred is possibly creating a heap of trouble.* I truly didn't expect anything, but Bob does things in very unusual ways, and I figured this was one of those very unusual times.

During the next three days we slipped, sludged, and inched our way toward Bastogne staying at least seven or eight miles ahead of Patton's lead units; thus, avoiding contact with the enemy was not always possible.

Janette was holding up exceedingly well and the men of Recon 1 had already started accepting her as one of their own. They all loved her. She was always upbeat and friendly, like an older sister to most of them.

At night, bundled up in our blankets, while laying next to her in a pup tent was not always the easiest thing I ever had to do but fortunately, or was it unfortunately, the weather was so damn cold, it offered few meaningful choices. I did always manage a kiss or two and told myself, *Oh, if only another place in another time*. I figured no one would ever know for sure what went on in here at night, and I wasn't going to be providing any clues.

Lieutenant Fred Mitchell with Bazooka
on the Road to Bastogne
December 1944

Staff Sergeant Dieter Troutner of Recon 1,

Road to Bastogne

December 1944

Tank Attachment of Recon 1, Road to Bastogne

December 1944

At 1015 on 21 December near the small village of Koench we ran headlong into a German armored patrol. We had no time to call for help. It was a stand and fight, may the best man win sorta thing. Neither had surprise on their side, both had reasonable cover, and each was evenly matched in both manpower and firepower.

Our two Sherman's were blasting away as fast as their gunners could load their 75's when in a flash of flames and smoke our lead tank exploded. There was nothing any of us could do except watch in horror as Recon 1 had just lost four brave members in a single moment of a thunderous explosion.

Meanwhile four members of our attached infantry squad, took two bazookas and circled, one to the north, one to the south, and got behind the two German armored vehicles. In coordination they both blasted the Germans with almost simultaneous barrages of missiles. In a flash of noisy, flaming explosions the score became two to one in our favor. We got both armored cars with a loss of everyone inside them which more than evened things up.

At the same time the rest of us were quite adequately holding our own. Fortunately when the Germans saw their armor destroyed, they had enough and left the field. We counted German losses at two armored vehicles, six dead and 1 seriously wounded. Our losses were one Sherman, 4 dead, 3 wounded, one seriously, yet Bastogne was still 20 miles away.

Unfortunately that wasn't all the bad news. Sergeant Kenton of our remaining Sherman reported he was all but out of gasoline, had only two rounds left for the 75mm gun, and was out of 50 caliber ammo for the machine guns. Adding to our misery, the jeeps attached to our infantry squad reported they were also low on gas.

Well, Fred, ole boy, another difficult decision to make. We could not just wait here; thus, I ordered the second tank destroyed, its attached infantry squad along with the remaining tankers to head back and rejoin Third Army, leaving Recon 1 with the original three jeeps, eleven combat ready men, and one lady.

Before our tankers and attached infantrymen left we transferred our few remaining fuel jerry cans to their jeeps along with our extra rations and ammo as we knew we were soon destined to become guests of the Germans. But until that happened Recon 1 would continue to keep Third Army informed. We then just watched solemnly as our support disappeared around the bend.

It was now 1430 hours, we were alone, worn out, and hungry. Dusk would be here shortly. The only hope for us which remained was somehow we might reach American lines. Our leaving with the others had never been an option. Recon 1 was still Third Army's advanced point, so we radioed headquarters of our status, pitched our tents, and ate cold C-rations. Tonight it was cold spam and potatoes. The grease had congealed into a gluey mess, but we needed the calories so we ate and dreamed it was filet mignon.

I told my men they had done a great job today, that we were getting close to Bastogne, get to bed, and hunker down. Staff Sergeant Troutner assigned picket duty. Reveille would be at 0400.

Janette and I retired to the "plush quarters" of my pup tent, I put my arm around her, kissed her softly, and said, "You are one delightful lady, Janette. Perhaps this time in which we are trudging along is not ready for someone as lovely and noble as you, and my eyes are seeing you from a time *which exists 56 years from now.* Today's present is like living in two times simultaneously. You will forever be in my memory, dear lady. You, and the soldiers I have been associated with here, will always be marching by my side for as long as God lets me reside on this earth. And, yes, someday, should fate allow it, perhaps, perhaps we *shall* meet once again in yet another more peaceful time." I kissed her first on the forehead and then gently on her lips. And dearest

Janette, darling Janette, please don't try to understand what I have just told you; for I can not give you any answers except that your vision will always travel with me.... I love you."

She replied, "Fred, you are so gallant and handsome too. I am certain, Sir, you are truly a *Ritter* (Knight) visiting us from another time, and *yes* we shall meet again someday. I shall miss you dearly, and Fred, I love you too." I was very pleased but reasoned, *in my dirty and battered condition after all this time on the line, it took real courage for her to say that.*

Corporal Ford, one of our pickets, and our radioman arrived at 0400. Excitedly he called, "Lieutenant, we have panzers immediately to our front and I think there is German Infantry with them and, Sir, they are coming straight at us!" I said, "Corporal, get everyone up and in place to abandon this area immediately." I had no thoughts that the eleven of us could do anything about the advancing panzers that we could so easily now hear. Janette had thrown off her blankets and was wide awake. She said, "You lead and I will be right behind you, Fred."

I grabbed the radio and transmitted to headquarters, "Emergency alert, this is Recon 1. German tanks are moving east to west to both the north and south of us. We are completely surrounded and our issue is totally hopeless.

Our tanks are both out of commission and my attached infantry, along with our wounded, left last evening to make contact with you. In all probability this will be Recon 1's final message, goodbye and over."

All I heard for a few moments was static, then, "Recon 1, your message received and understood. Good show, Recon 1, good show. Do whatever you need to do in accordance with your situation, over and out." That was it. Now once more…only static. Effectively we had just been written off…. We were expendable.

I said, "Corporal Ford, destroy the radio." And then turned to Sergeant Troutner, "Have hand grenades placed on the engine mounts of our jeeps, and upon my order pull their pins. Then have the men wrap their rifles around tree trunks. And, Sergeant, at first light you and I will show the white flag. I have a plan in mind which involves Janette and am certain she will approve of it."

At 0530 as daylight was arriving, Sergeant Troutner and I rigged white flags onto a couple long poles. We stood up in plain sight and began waving them, saying loudly in German. "We want to *sich besprechen (*confer) with your commanding officer." Shortly two Germans appeared to our front and shouted, in English, "Come on over, Yank." Sergeant Troutner and I trudged forward through the deepening snow until we met face to face with Major Erik Hoffman and Feldwebel (Sergeant) Max Klinger of the 3rd Battalion, 5th Panzer Army. *We were in luck, this was General von Manteuffel's command.*

I saluted, introduced myself and Staff Sergeant Troutner, and immediately made my offer.

"Major I am prepared to surrender the men of Reconnaissance Squad 1, Third United States Army, and I have one extremely important request.... I have a personal message for General von Manteuffel and assure you he will want to hear it directly from me. Secondly, Madame Janette Marie von Kluge the daughter-in-law of Field Marshall von Kluge is a guest of mine. Madame von Kluge is a family friend of Frau and Herr General von Manteuffel. Shall I ask her to be brought forward, Sir?"

Major Hoffman was stunned, but soon collected himself and replied, "Lieutenant this is a most unusual request. Yes, please have Madame von Kluge brought forward." I waved my white flag and as we had pre-planed, Private First Class Hepburn and Madame von Kluge appeared from behind the trees and trudged through the snow toward us.

As she neared, Major Hoffman stiffened to attention, saluted, and said, "Madame von Kluge what a distinct pleasure this is. I am honored to have served on the Eastern Front with your late husband, Oberst (Colonel) von Kluge. I am so sorry for his demise."

Janette Marie nodded and as if to ignore me replied without even a glance my way, "Thank you Major for your concern. Now I would like to be taken at once to see General von Manteuffel. I am very cold and very hungry." He quickly answered, "At once, Madame von Kluge."

He turned to Feldwebel Klinger and ordered him to have his command car brought to him immediately. When it arrived he ordered Klinger to take Troutner and me to headquarters and hold us there until he received further orders. He then sped off with Janette; now, all we could do was wait. Fortunately when we arrived at 5th Panzer Headquarters we were fed and allowed to use their latrines.

At around 1300 Major Hoffman returned and asked me to come with him. He said, "Well, Lieutenant, apparently you are to speak with the General. I do not understand what influence Madame von Kluge had, but it must have been, as you Americans say, a doozie. Follow me, and you may bring your Sergeant with you if you wish." I did wish and we quickly followed Hoffman to his command car. It was only a short distance to von Manteuffel's headquarters.

General von Manteuffel wearing his Iron Cross
with Crossed Swords and Diamonds
(Highest Order of Ritterkreuze)
1944

General con Manteuffel with aide,

Major Kraemer, Ardennes,

December 1944

General von Manteuffel, near Bastogne

December 1944

As we arrived General von Manteuffel was seated at a field desk in a well lighted, pleasantly warm, but otherwise stark command tent. As we entered he stood and I recognized him immediately. Younger, but very much the same appearance as when I met him at his home in Diessen for the first time in 1969 during my 2000 timeline. Small in stature, but with those steely blue eyes he commanded his surroundings and his reputation as a panzer general was only equaled by Panzer Generals Hans Guderian and Erwin Rommel. Staff Sergeant Troutman and I stood erect, at attention in front of him, and saluted. I spoke. "Herr General von Manteuffel, how good of you to see us. I will need a private meeting with you, Sir, for what I have to tell you is for your ears only."

I waited as he looked at me rather seriously with his steely blue eyes, and had time to realize *that since 1969 had not arrived yet by his timeline, he would know nothing of my future visit with him.* He finally, sternly replied, "Lieutenant, it is because of Madame von Kluge's glowing praise of your handling of her and other German prisoners that I grant you this." *Oops, hadn't exactly considered her a prisoner, but under these circumstances, guessed that was OK.* I simply said, "Thank you, Sir." He ushered everyone else from his command tent ordering Major Hoffman to make sure this area remained secure.

When we were alone, General von Manteuffel, who spoke good English, seated himself behind his desk and asked me to sit in a chair facing him. I was nervous. Even though I had practiced in my mind what to say, crunch time was now upon me like a cold damp blanket and it was scary. I had to say something and it had better be an attention getter.

So my saga began, "General von Manteuffel, please, Sir, allow me to finish what I am going to tell you. I am certain you will be tempted to question it." He nodded his agreement and replied, "Of course, Lieutenant, please continue."

I said, "Thank you, Sir.... *Herr General, I am a visitor from the year 2000.*" I waited and watched, but his facial expression did not change, so I just continued. "The only proof I have is to tell you my wife, Shirley, and I will visit you and Frau Armgard von Kliest several times in the years to come at your home in Diessen am Ammersee, south of Munich.

"I know a lot about you, Sir. For instance, you believed your future wife to be the most beautiful blue-eyed blonde you had ever met, you were married to her on 23 June 1921, and you have two children. And, Sir, you were promoted to your current rank over several senior generals by the Fuhrer on 2 September, 1944. You are a devotee of the card game, bridge, and at your meeting with Hitler in November 1944 concerning the Ardennes offensive preparations, you suggested he try for a *kliener schlag* (small slam) instead of a *grosser schlag* (grand slam). However, your advice was not heeded.

"Further, I could tell you of your successes after this war has ended, and as you know, it will end soon. But

I will not do this. I ask only that you remember me for as I say, we shall meet again. I know of these things for I have studied your history from the vantage point of the future."

General der Panzer Truppen, Hasso Eccard von Manteuffel, sat upright and looked directly at me; his crystal blue eyes cut a hole right through me. I was not sure as to how my presentation went, but I too sat solidly upright, looked straight at him, and prayed he would believe my sincerity.

His reply startled me.... "Time traveler, you say? An interesting subject, Lieutenant." His demeanor now seemed more relaxed and he continued. "I have discussed the possibilities of time travel on several occasions with Werner von Braun, one of Germany's leading rocket scientists. He contends some day time travel will be accomplished, and if I am to believe you, Lieutenant, it has been." Without flinching, I simply answered, "Yes, Sir, it has."

General von Manteuffel continued, “Well, Lieutenant Mitchell, what do you propose I do with you?” Rather surprised I answered, “Well, Sir, tomorrow is Christmas Eve, and you must know General Patton’s leading Corps is arriving on your southern flank as we speak, and in all probability you will be on the defensive by morning. Herr Hitler’s *grosser schlag* has achieved all it is going to.

“Therefore, Sir, I ask in the spirit of *Weinachten*, you release me and my men through your lines toward Bastogne. My small contingent is totally exhausted and we can only be a burden to you. Also, I am certain it would be a gesture of gallantry which Madame von Kluge would appreciate, and which would become a living part of your legacy remembered in the future history of this conflict, Sir.” For the first time the General smiled broadly and continued, “Interesting recommendation, Lieutenant, and boldly presented too. I like that; it is similar to an idea given to me by Madame von Kluge. She really thinks highly of you, Lieutenant, and your honesty and forthrightness is appreciated.

"By the way, this conversation should and shall remain our secret. Frau von Manteuffel and I will look forward to your future visits. If, by chance you see General Patton, please tell him of my respect and interest in his reincarnations, also that I hope to visit with him after the war."

Von Manteuffel called for Major Hoffman who soon presented himself and he ordered, "Major, tomorrow morning at daybreak, personally escort Lieutenant Mitchell and his men to the frontline at Bastogne, contact the Americans, and release them as a token of our common celebration of this most holy day, and add, *Frohe Weinachten* (Merry Christmas)."

I could tell Major Hoffman was surprised, perhaps shocked, but at the same time he seemed pleased with the order he had just received; he offered no reply other than, "Yes, Herr General, at once." He then smiled at me and said, "Follow me, *Ober Leutnant* (First Lieutenant)." As I was leaving, I stopped, turned around, stood erect, and saluted saying only, "Sir!" Manteuffel replied, "*Auf wiedersehen, Herr Ober Leutnant.*" I turned and followed Hoffman.

* * * * *

Christmas Eve, 24 December, 1944 arrived, cold, but rather clear for the first time in several days. At 0600 at the front near Bastogne, Major Hoffman walked to the edge of the woods and waved a white flag. It was answered by another white flag carried by two American officers, a Captain Carpenter and Lieutenant Smith of the 101st Airborne.

The two sides met in an opening between the lines and shortly Major Hoffman waved his arms in a come here motion and that was the signal for us, the eleven spent men of Recon 1, to be brought forward. When we arrived, Major Hoffman said to the American officers, "Gentlemen I present you with Lieutenant Fred Mitchell and his reconnaissance men. A *Weinachten* present from General Hasso von Manteuffel."

As a result of General McAuliffe's recent reply of *Nuts* to the Germans recent demand that Bastogne be surrendered, Captain Carpenter and Lieutenant Smith were completely taken by surprise.

Finally, Captain Carpenter regained his composure and replied, "Major, this is an unparalleled surprise. But I must say it is sure within the spirit of Christmas. On behalf of our General McAuliffe we thank you, Sir. Please present our Christmas wishes to General von Manteuffel."

Everyone saluted and Recon 1 trudged back through the snow to the American lines. Major Hoffman disappeared into the woods from where we had come. We were all thankful to be free, if you can call it free, while being still surrounded by the German 5th Panzer Army.

It was so strange hearing Christmas music in the distance. We were hurried off to headquarters and interrogated by a Major Franks of intelligence, but we were so tired, dirty, and hungry we were barely coherent. Finally our little group was fed, and bedded down in a bombed out house. It had no windows, and only a partial roof over our heads, but it was Christmas and it would hopefully be a place where we could finally find sleep, peace and quiet not required, only sleep.

We awoke on Christmas morning still not fully realizing we were free. The day arrived clear and cold, and we heard considerable commotion coming from the north, south, and east as if something big was happening. The noise continued unabated until late afternoon when our pickets reported no German activity could be heard or seen anywhere.

Our wonderment was answered on 26 December when the first tanks of Patton's lead division began to appear from the south of Bastogne. Apparently all the noise we had heard was the German withdrawal to the east. It was definitely the beginning of the end for Hitler's *Grosse Schlag*.

Recon 1 was returned to our headquarters unit which had just arrived at Bastogne. We were different people than those who departed from Metz only nineteen very long days ago on 7 December, 1944. It seemed to us like our lives had changed forever and we were certain they had.

On 27 December Recon 1 was commended for its patrol from Metz to Bastogne by Brigadier General McAuliffe of the 101st Airborne, the Commanding Officer at Bastogne. He advised we would be returning to Metz for some well deserved rest and relaxation. We were jubilant. All anyone could think of was food, beer, hot baths, girls, and sleep. All not necessarily in that order of importance.

However, before we were to leave I was summoned to meet with General Patton. I had no idea as to why until I was advised by General McAuliffe that I would be receiving the Silver Star Medal with a V for valor.

Now I was really stunned, but soon recovered and asked General McAuliffe to please arrange for me to have a private audience with General Patton as I had some personal information for him from General von Manteuffel.

General McAuliffe said he would inquire, and in about an hour he returned and told me my private meeting with Patton was arranged for on 28 December at 0930. This left me scant time to prepare.

My day arrived and I was ushered into General Patton's command tent by his aide, Colonel Mark Jacobson. The General stood looking every bit what I had expected including his ivory handled pistol strapped at his side. Yeh, I was impressed. I saluted.

He returned my salute and in a firm voice said, "Lieutenant Mitchell, I am proud to make your acquaintance, please be seated." He continued, "Lieutenant, I have reviewed the record of your unit's endeavors over the last three weeks and find it an outstanding example of what I expect from my people. That is why *I am awarding you the Silver Star with a V.* And in addition all members of Recon 1 will be awarded a unit citation ribbon."

I was speechless. Never in my wildest dreams did I expect this. General Patton smiled which helped. Finally, I gulped a reply. "Sir, thank you on behalf of all my men, including those tankers who joined us until they ran out of ammo. They paid a high price for their efforts and I sincerely hope they too are to take part in this honor." Without hesitation General Patton replied, "Yes, yes, of course, Lieutenant. They will be included."

I replied, "Thank you, Sir, and may I speak freely?" General Patton grinned, "Hell yes, Lieutenant, wouldn't have it any other God damn way. Let her rip, son."

"General Patton, Sir, I am aware of your absolute belief in reincarnation and I believe what you say is true. Sir, you see, I too have traveled in time, and am now but a visitor here today. Believe me or not, the choice, Sir, is yours. However, I want you to know I was most fascinated by your presence at the Battle of Thermopylae in 480 BC where, under the leadership of the Persian Xerxes, you helped destroy the Spartan Army under the command of Leonidas. And General Patton, Sir, the poem you wrote regarding your belief in reincarnation is my favorite. Embarrassed that I don't recall the title, I know the poem by heart. If you please, Sir:

"Through the travail of the ages,
Midst the pomp and toil of war,
Have I fought and strove and perished
Countless times upon this star.
So as through a glass, and darkly
The age long strife I see
Where I fought in many guises,
Many names, but always me.
So forever in the future,
Shall I battle as of yore,
Dying to be born a fighter,
But to die again, once more."

General Patton sat quietly looking down for quite some time. In fact, so long, I was becoming concerned I had done or said something out of line; thus, I just sat nervously and waited.

After what seemed to me like a decade, he raised his head, looked straight at me, and said, "Mitchell, that was one of the finest renditions I have ever heard; further, am impressed and pleased in all respects with what you have said. Of course I believe you, son. Wish we had more time to talk, but guess we still have a war to finish." I answered, "Yes we do, Sir. But General, if you will permit me I do have one more important thing to tell you on behalf of your opponent, General von Manteuffel.

"You know, Sir, Recon 1 was a prisoner of his until he released us as a Christmas gesture on Christmas Eve. General von Manteuffel is, as you are, Sir, every bit a cavalier and a gallant gentleman"

The General quickly replied, "Go ahead, I am anxious to hear what he had to say." I continued, "In my conversation with him I was able to tell him I had traveled in time from the year 2000 to take part in this battle, and was amazed he was impressed with that fact. Seems he is interested in the possibilities of time travel and was quick to point out that you, Sir, are an advocate of reincarnation. I was impressed he knew of you in such detail.

"After he told me of our impending release back to American lines, he asked me to relay greetings and this message to you. He said, 'Tell General Patton his army is blessed to have within it's ranks both a person reincarnate and also a time traveler. It would be my pleasure and hope to someday meet him. My best wishes.' "

Patton broadly smiled, saying, "Damn, I am impressed with you and your report as well of the tidings you bring from General von Manteuffel. I have one more bit of news for you." He got up, walked to the door of his command tent, hollered, "Colonel Jacobson, come inside."

When Jacobson entered Patton said bluntly, "Cut orders immediately promoting First Lieutenant Mitchell to Captain effective this date, get two pairs of captain bars, take Captain Mitchell with you, and see he gets back to his men. And, Colonel Jacobson, please pin the bars on the Captain on my behalf." Colonel Jacobson replied, "Yes, Sir." General Patton stood, said, "Mitchell, it has been great, I damn well wish I had a thousand more like you." Colonel Jacobson and I saluted, turned, and departed.

My brain was in a turmoil; I simply couldn't believe what had happened to me. In about a half hour Colonel Jacobson called me into his office and removed my silver lieutenant bar, replacing it with silver twin bars denoting my new rank of captain. Then we got into his jeep and drove to where Recon 1 was waiting for whatever news I might bring.

As we approached the location where Recon 1 was located, they were all lined up awaiting my arrival. As I got out of the jeep Colonel Jacobson said, "So long, Captain Mitchell. Please pass on to your men General Patton's thanks for a job well done." I replied, "Yes, Sir, I will, and thank you, Sir." He returned my salute, threw another toward the men of Recon 1, and drove away. My intrepid little group had noticed my captain's bars and began to hurrah me in their usual vociferous way. They were loud, but I could tell they were proud and pleased.

I issued my first command as a captain...."Fall in!" Then immediately ordered, "Stand at rest, I have some very important things to tell you. First, General Patton sends his personal thanks for the job you did, and he has ordered a unit citation to Recon 1 which will include our support tank attachment group as well. I only wish all of them could be present in person, but I know they will be here in spirit.

"Further, you are aware that I have been awarded the Silver Star Medal with a V. I am honored beyond belief, but I feel exceedingly humbled. I shall never, never wear it without acknowledging *it belongs to each and every one of you wonderful guys as much as it belongs to me. Thanks, I love you. Dismissed!*" Everyone shook my hand, one at a time, saying, "We thank you, Sir."

This was a very moving event for me and as I walked away from my band of brothers I realized my time here in France was limited. Bob would be awaiting my call to return to the 21st century.

If you could believe it I was saddened by the thought of leaving before this terrible war ended, though I realized the end was still 4½ months away. What I had seen and done was beyond my ability to totally comprehend. Even my experiences at Pearl Harbor didn't fully prepare me for the on-the-ground experiences of war that I received here. When I get home I'll be 82, and perhaps that is good, for my life has been changed for whatever time there is left to me. I am not saddened, just not certain what those life changes will mean.

I had told my unit I had to leave for awhile and would be gone for a couple of weeks or so. That of course was a lie, but I had no real way to tell them I was a traveler in time and was leaving them, returning to the year 2000. I felt so unusual, perhaps a little bit like being a deserter.

After I first disappeared from camp they would list me as being absent without leave (AWOL). Probably later as missing in action (MIA), and finally missing and presumed dead. In time, thus would close the presence here in France of one, Captain Fred D. Mitchell. Alone with my thoughts I finally said to myself, *Ok, Bob, I am ready. Get the Train to Perpetuity rolling.*

* * * * *

As Bob and I had planned I found a secluded place at the edge of a wooded area nearby to await the *Train to Perpetuity.* Still dressed in my beat up army combat uniform, and carrying my M-1 rifle, I called, "OK, Bob, come and get me." I knew Bob would be zeroed in and quickly be able to locate me.

Didn't have to wait long before the *Train to Perpetuity* materialized. The conductor got off and as he always did placed the step for me to get on, and Bob said, "Welcome back, Lieutenant, oh excuse me, Captain. Did you have fun?" I answered, "Oh, my God, Bob, this was an unbelievable experience. I don't think I will ever recover from this one." He chuckled lightly, "Yeh, Fred, think I have heard that one before." Next I heard the conductor call, "All aboard, all aboard!" Makes me laugh every time I hear him do that; no one else can hear him.

I asked Bob how long I been away and he told me only three days had passed in 2000 time. That was great. Shirley was away visiting family and wouldn't even miss me.

Bob handed me a mirror and it was reality time again. No 26 year old kid now! Ugh, just like after my trip to Pearl Harbor! I said, "Thank you, Bob. I'm glad I did it, but as usual, I am glad to be home."

The conductor brought me a cold beer and a ham and cheese sandwich with some potato chips. That really hit the spot and as I sat, nibbled, and looked out my window the *Train to Perpetuity* began to journey down the mythical tracts ahead to the year 2000. It chugged, hissed steam from it's boiler, and thick black smoke curled once more like a giant reptile from it's smokestack. Soon the scenery warped, as it always does, into that familiar blue haze as we crossed time continuums.

I inquired if I could keep my M-1 rifle and my uniform? Bob smiled that great big toothy smile of his, "For heaven's sake, Fred, with all the stuff you have brought back from your other adventures, you should open a war museum, but of course you can."

* * * * *

Bob then added, "Now listen up, Fred, here comes the big one. It has to do with your visits to Diessen, Germany when you and Shirley visited von Manteuffel during your 2000 timeline.

"However, you have not visited there during your new 1944 timeline. Therefore, in order for you and Shirley to experience them, the *Train to Perpetuity* will stop in Diessen for you to retake your 1969, 1972, 1974, and 1977 visits.... I will arrange for Shirley to be with you in order for her also to become a part of your 1944 timeline visits.... Fred, it will be similar to *creating two separate files* on your computer. One file will be the 1944 timeline and the other the 2000 timeline. They will exist side by side but separate to each other. After your visits are complete, you and Shirley will only recall your lives as they exist in your new 1944 timeline.... Got it?"

Initially I was astonished and still a little confused. The thought of visiting von Manteuffel at Diessen a second time? But after due thought Bob's logic began to make sense and said, "OK, let's get on with it." Bob, I have one more question, How in the world will you get Shirley here? She's in Illinois in the year 2000 visiting family."

Bob replied, "Not to worry, ole buddy, Shirley and you will continue on in your 2000 timeline world, as if your 1944 experience never happened. But Shirley and you *will also* be chugging away in your new 1944 timeline, quite oblivious to your 2000 timeline. The Fred and Shirley who are here will remember only the 1944 timeline....but out there somewhere in the universe, perhaps even very near you....in your parallel 2000 world there will also be a Fred and Shirley who will not be aware of the 1944 timeline. Neat, huh? See what ya got to look forward to in your future work." (At the end of my time travel to Pearl Harbor, I had been told by Bob I would someday become an angel guiding time travelers).

I said to myself, *of course, why didn't I think of that?* He amazes me…*That kind of logic from an itinerate ole cowboy from the 1880's.*

PART 5

WORLD OF PARALLEL TIMELINES

1944 "New" and 2000 "Old"

In accordance with Bob's instructions to update our trip home with our "new" 1944 timeline, the *Train to Perpetuity* made four stops at Diessen, Germany. Each stop *individually* replaced our original 2000 timeline visits that Shirley and I had made to Frau and General von Manteuffel at their home between 1969 and 1977.

General at Home

During each of our "new" 1944 timeline update stops the General escorted us, as he had done on our original visits during our "old" 2000 timeline, to Munich and various other places.

However, this time the General and I were now once more together on the same timeline and we could recall our common experience at Bastogne as they had occurred in 1944. Thus, we spent a lot of time reminiscing the events which occurred during that fateful time. We agreed it was a *Damn Cold December…* during *Weinachten* (Christmas) 1944.

During my revisit of 1969 General von Manteuffel recalled he had not been able to meet General Patton due to his unfortunate death in an automobile accident in Bavaria during late December 1945. I thought it interesting the General recalled telling me of his wish to visit Patton while I was a prisoner in his tent.

Additionally, the General had said, "Fred, I remember you as a young American Lieutenant taken prisoner by my command who, along with your patrol, was accompanied by a friend of our family, one Madame Janette Maria von Kluge. Because of her request, and because I was impressed by your sincerity, I released you and your patrol back to American lines on Christmas Eve 1944." I smiled, looked straight at the General and answered, "General von Manteuffel, Sir, yes, you have a good memory of those events which took place so long ago, and *Sir, I am that person and I recall informing you I was a time traveler."*

He seemed pleased, his steely crystal blue eyes still sparkled as he said, "Yes, yes, you did tell me, and you said you would see me again in the years to come. Frau von Manteuffel and I are very pleased you and Shirley are here." We continued to talk about my sudden appearance in his command tent. Shirley and Frau von Manteuffel sat in amazement as we unfolded the details of our meeting near Bastogne on that cold Christmas Eve in 1944.

* * * * *

A little later I changed the subject and inquired of the General about Madame von Kluge's whereabouts. He smiled as he informed me she had married a Baron Herman Klausen and lived nearby in Augsburg. He recalled his surprise and delight when I brought Janette von Kluge to him.

He then provided me with her telephone number and asked if I should like to call her. To which I replied, "Yes, Sir, I would very much like to see her if that is at all possible." Before calling, I reasoned, *Let's see, I am now 51, so Maria would be 59.* She would certainly remember me, but pondered *what would her reaction be to hearing from me so suddenly after 25 years?*

I thought, *Well, here goes.* Nervously I dialed the number. One ring, two rings, three rings, and finally a female voice answered, "*Frau Klausen.*" I felt weak kneed, but took a deep breathe and quickly regained myself. "Janette, Janette Maria, this is Lieutenant Fred Mitchell and I am calling you from General von Manteuffel's home in Diessen."

After a considerable delay she answered, "Fred! Oh, *mein Gott in himmel*, is it really you?" To which I answered, "Yes, Janette, it is and Mrs. Mitchell is here with me. May we come calling?" Janette, without pause replied, "Yes, yes, of course, dear Fred. Would tomorrow be too soon?" Of course it was fine with me. As it was only a short trip from where we were staying in Diessen, I asked if ten o'clock in the morning would be all right. She immediately responded, "Yes, yes, dear, Fred. We'll have coffee and lunch."

The next morning Shirley and I arrived at Janette's Augsburg address. An estate which to my amazement looked dramatically similar to the Château where she had lived in France back in 1944. I approached with some trepidation and rang the bell on the front door. When the door opened, there stood Janette Marie looking much as she did 25 years ago. Only a few streaks of gray now graced her hair. She had tears in her eyes, and as I saw her, I too developed a few.

The years had been good to both of us and from the moment we first looked into each others eyes it was apparent what we had experienced so many years ago had sealed an unbreakable bond between us. We both stood transfixed for a couple seconds. Then with enthusiasm we simultaneously threw our arms about each other, hugged, and kissed. An unpredictable, extremely spontaneous, and emotional moment was the only way to describe our meeting. Perhaps a bit of embarrassment for Shirley, but as a good trooper and somewhat accustomed to my novel reactions to my time travel situations, she never let on. I loved her so very much for it.

Shirley entered the great room first, and holding hands Janette and I followed. Again I marveled at how much this place reminded me of her old Château in France. Janette first showed us around her gracious manor and next we chatted back and forth on what we had done over the course of the last twenty-five years. Her marriage in 1949 to Baron Klausen, their move to Augsburg, my marriage to Shirley in 1952 and working for AT&T (American Telephone and Telegraph). I presented General von Manteuffel's greeting to her as well.

Next we dined, sitting leisurely at a large solid mahogany table, beneath a magnificent candelabra, and served by a uniformed maid. During lunch Janette and I began to relive our journey to Bastogne during that cold December of 1944. We talked and laughed about everything in great detail, missing nothing. It was very emotional for us both, and bless Shirley, she continued to sit quietly by sipping on a glass of great German *Liebfraumilch* wine.

After a little more than three hours we began our farewells. Janette asked when we would be returning and I replied, "Janette Marie, I do not know if or when we might return. This has been an unbelievable occasion and perhaps we are both better off retaining our memories as they are now."

Janette looked somewhat sad and tears streaked her still lovely cheeks. She replied, "Yes, Fred, you are perhaps right. In any event, I shall never forget you nor let your memory fade. We, Sir, are kindred spirits joined now only in memory by the passage of time, right?"…. I thought her reply was tremendous and right on target. I simply added, "Yes, Janette, we are truly that." I pulled her to me, kissed her with some emotion, and said, "Goodbye, Janette Marie, goodbye."

Shirley and I then left; she has never asked of me any more questions. Obviously she believed me when I told her I had given her all the facts regarding my personal relations with Janette. And once again I had occasion to love and respect her.

This ended our "new" 1944 timeline visit with the General for the year 1969. In order to complete updating all of our visits, we still had three more stops to make to Diessen before finally chugging our way aboard the *Train To Perpetuity* to the year 2000. At each ensuing stop we were escorted to various points of interest by the General, and sometimes Frau Manteuffel accompanied us. We always had ample time to continue our reflections about Bastogne.

After completing our visits Bob and the *Train to Perpetuity* were waiting nearby to take us back to the desert near Tortilla Flat, Arizona; our trip was finally over. I collected my souvenirs and Shirley and I got off the *train* near where I had parked my car.

We said goodbye to Bob, the conductor, and the fireman. Then watched as the *Train to Perpetuity* chugged, hissed, blew smoke, as she faded once again into the distant mists of time. Wondering if we should ever see her again?

Somehow I rather doubted it. However I did wonder, if I do become an angel mentor to time travelers, *what will my conveyance be?*

* * * * *

We drove straight home, not stopping at Big John's for a drink. I had already decided that for awhile this trip was going to be mine and Shirley's alone because we had so much to chew on.

I simply said to Shirley, "Someday perhaps soon, I will talk with Big John about this trip, but not right now. I just want to get home and get things back to somewhere near normal, if that is even possible." Shirley answered she understood and I sincerely hoped she did.

What an experience this had been! Shirley and I had completed our "new" 1944 timeline visits. Now our "old" 2000 timeline, we supposed, was traveling along beside us somewhere out there, or so Bob had led us to believe, each world oblivious to the other.

PART 6

EPILOGUE

General von Manteuffel was a gracious host to the end which came on 24 September, 1978 at the age of 81. Mrs. Mitchell and I received an invitation to his funeral and prior to that in 1969 we had also been invited to attend the 30th anniversary of the formation of the Gross Deutschland Division. General von Manteuffel, then a Colonel, was the division's first commander.

Unfortunately because of business reasons which at the time I felt were important, we did not attend either. To this day I have been eternally sorry I let business-of-the-day reasons stand above attending these events. Yet am certain that General von Manteuffel has graciously forgiven me.

However, in 2001 Shirley and I returned to visit his gravesite at Diessen. It was a very moving time for me and for Shirley as well. As I stood transfixed beside his gravesite, tears dampened my cheeks and my handkerchief. It seemed to me an eternal visitation that brought home some very vivid and personal memories; such as, our several visits with the General and Frau von Manteuffel at their home in Diessen, and also the correspondence which the General and I maintained from our first visit in 1969 until his death.

Shirley finally tapped me gently on the shoulder and said, "Fred, it's time now to go." Slowly, but deliberately, I took two steps backward, stood rigidly erect, saluted, and said, *"Yes, Herr General, my old friend, now you belong to the ages. Auf wiedersehen."* I was still sobbing as

I turned, took Shirley by the hand, and we silently left his resting place.

I felt so hollow inside. Now all I have left are my photographs, and the dozens of letters which passed between us. I occasionally still reread them. It is difficult for me to explain why I felt so close to this man, but no matter, I did.

January 3, 1972

Dear General von Manteuffel,

I hope this first letter of the New Year finds everything fine in Diessen. Our weather here remains unusually warm. We have as yet had no snow. Our Christmas was fine. The children as usual had a fine day.

Your trip to West Point in March sounds interesting. Will Mrs. von Manteuffel be coming with you? Herr General, you know that if you can continue your trip to Chicago, Mrs Mitchell and I would enjoy very much your visit. I would be glad to show you some of the interesting sights of Chicago.

I hope your visit with Herr Speer goes well. If Mrs. Mitchell and I visit in Germany in May, we still hope to visit with him.

We read in the papers that there are still some problems in the new travel agreement between West and East Germany. Do you think this agreement will really work?

What are your opinions about the recent devaluation of the Dollar? Will it affect West Germany's economy? What is the reaction of the public? I know that it will certainly affect the cost of my trips to Europe. However we are still planning our trip for sometime in May.

Thank you for describing your involvement in Africa. Did you ever have an occasion to meet Rommel? It seems Rommel was able to develop a great reputation. I'm certain that it was deserved. Did the Allies occasionally over react to this reputation?

Mrs. Mitchell and I want to wish you a very happy Birthday on January 14. Will you be doing anything special this year?

Please also give to Mrs. von Manteuffel our best wishes as always.

Your friend,

Fred

H.v.Manteuffel.   8918) Diessen / A.
March 17 th 1974.

Dear Fred,

that was a very good information by your kind letter March 13 th-we are very glad to meet you here in Diessen/ A (with Mrs. and Mr. David)-we are between May 12 and 20 at home! I wait for your further information when your touring is fixed! Give me, please, your ideas if you wish to order for lodging in this area (room or two rooms?).-I have to thank you for your very kind letter Febr. 5 th-but I ask for your indulgence-I have to work in these weeks with the corrections of my biography and another working out(my co-operation on a encyclopaedia).

Our grandchild (in Persia/ Iran) has her second baby-the little boy is delighted to have a sister and a playmate!

We are looking forward with greatest pleasure, dear Fred!

With warmest remembrances and very best wishes for a good flight

in friendship Yours

H.v.Manteuffel

November 7, 1975

Dear General von Manteuffel,

I am writing you just a short letter today to let you know how very pleased Mrs. Mitchell and I were to receive your correspondence. We were sorry to hear that you had been ill, but hope that by now you are feeling well and enjoying a beautiful Bavarian fall season.

We have just received your book, and look forward with great pleasure to reading it. I am sure that I will have a lot of questions to ask of you afterwards.

Is the book going to be translated in German?

The weather remains warm here. We are surprised at how much milder the fall and winter season are here in comparison to Chicago.

We vacationed this year in New England and Canada. We had a very enjoyable time, but would rather have gone to Europe. Everything is so expensive (rooms, meals, gasoline,etc.).

Lynne was glad that you asked of her and told me to send her best wishes. She remembers with pleasure her visit to Diessen.

I'm leaving tomorrow on business to Chicago, so I'll be able to visit our son and his wife. It's always nice to go home for a visit.

We read with interest about the great robbery at the Koln Cathedral.

This will be all for now, but I will write again soon after reading "Panzer Baron".

With sincere best wishes and warmest regards, your friend,

Hasso von Manteuffel

Dießen/Ammersee

im Januar 1977

Dear Fred and Mrs. Mitchell:

At my eighty birthday I received a great many of greeting cards and letters (185) that it is impossible to thank everybody at the time being - I ask for your forbearance! I am pleased with your honorable memory and thank you as is fitting!

Add to this I was in bed for some weeks and have to go in ahospital for scrutiny-deisease of the kidneys-
I hope to pass by an operation!

With kindest regards
in friendship
signed
v. Manteuffel

In January 2002 the telephone rang. It was Captain Benjamin Morris from the Air Force. He said, "Fred, I hope you and your family are well, been awhile since I visited you. I have something amazing to tell you. It involves your father, Lieutenant Mathew Mitchell." (Morris had visited me in 2000 when he brought dad's personal items to me).

I was speechless, but finally responded, "Yes, Sir." He continued, "Fred, I am flying tomorrow to Phoenix and would like to meet with you, Shirley, and any of your children who might be available. And by the way, Fred, I will be bringing with me a person who also has some information about your father. Could we meet at your home, say at 9:30 AM the day after tomorrow?" I responded quickly, "Yes, Sir, Shirley and I will look forward to your visit. I will see who else I can get here." Captain Morris said, "Fine, I'll see you at that time." I told Shirley, and we wondered what he wanted to tell us, and who he was bringing? I just shrugged my shoulders and said, "Don't have any idea, but I am excited."

We were unable to round up Fred Jr. and Lynne on such short notice; thus, we anxiously sat in anticipation of Captain Ben Morris's arrival. He arrived in a US Air Force staff car at exactly 0930 and we were surprised when we saw a very pretty blonde lady accompanying him. I just squinted at Shirley and grunted, "Hmm."

After introducing himself and Sandy Greer, Shirley offered us coffee and cookies which were graciously accepted. Captain Morris thanked her and began. "Fred, I have an amazing story to tell you and I may as well cut right to the core. Fred, your father, Lieutenant Mathew Mitchell, *was a traveler in time….* Also, he was a friend of mine. This is what happened." To say the least I was *surprised* and sat anxiously in anticipation!

Ben began, "In June 2000 Lieutenant Mitchell, flying his Sopwith Camel fighter plane, landed at our Air Force base at Pawtucket, Delaware. He, without any warning, just landed his plane; arriving there from France where he had been engaged in combat with German planes until a remarkable disappearance into a large cloud formation transported him unexplainably to Pawtucket. Lieutenant Mitchell remained with us only a few days before taking off in his Sopwith Camel and disappearing once again into a cloud formation. We, of course, just assumed he had crashed into the ocean.

"The story might have ended right there except for my curiosity. I asked the Air Force for his military records. It was then I learned he had somehow returned to Cerlot, France and was subsequently killed in action in June 1918.

"While in Pawtucket Mathew had the occasion to see how airpower had advanced from propeller powered planes made from paper, wood, and glue, to jets which exceeded speeds of 1500 mph. He was able to see aircraft from WWII and he took a flight in my Jet Interceptor where we did barrel rolls and other maneuvers. Mat was fascinated.

"Also while he was at Pawtucket, he had occasion to spend some time with Sandy. Sandy, please take over."

In a very pleasing voice, she began, "Fred and Shirley, thank you for allowing me to come along with Ben. It is an honor to meet you. The very remembrance of meeting your father brings me almost to tears.... I want you to know, Fred, how impressed I was with your father, and how pleased I am to be meeting his son. Your father was at all times a very gallant gentleman of the old school. On several occasions we danced, dined, walked in the moonlight, and talked endlessly about our respective times. At no time were his intentions or manners inappropriate or ill-intended. You should be very proud.

"It was an experience which potentially had the makings for a romance novel. My wish was that he remain with us, but he felt it would not be appropriate to do so... simply he wanted to return to his time and to his war. Now we know that he did."

Ben, said, "Thank you, Sandy" and continued. "During his stay with us in 2000 he had been asked if he would like a reunion with his family whom our staff had located. He declined it on the basis that it would add nothing but confusion for you, and to his memories of Connie. We didn't necessarily agree with him, but did agree to not tell you of his presence at Pawtucket in the year 2000." Captain Morris then proceeded to tell us, in great detail, of Lieutenant Mitchell's visit To Pawtucket. (*See Part 1*)

Ben continued to tell us how he and my father had become good friends. It was because of this he felt we deserved to know the truth, and believed First Lieutenant Mathew Dale Mitchell would forgive him for violating his pledge.

To say the least we were surprised, elated, and excited about what we had just been told. It was an amazing story, and one I could easily buy. I thanked Captain Morris and Sandy, and told them I was certain dad would be glad they told us his story. It must have been heart rendering for dad to decline a reunion and we will respect his memory, even more, for his feelings.

I said, "Ben, it seems only fair that I tell you something.... I too have traveled in time: *The Hindenburg in May 1937, Pearl Harbor on 7 December, 1941, and Battle of the Bulge in 1944."* Ben and Sandy were at first taken aback, but recovered nicely and Ben replied, "Well, why am I not surprised? Guess it runs in the family."

I provided Captain Morris and Sandy Greer each with signed copies of my books covering my visits back in time. They said they greatly appreciated them and would share them with others back at Pawtucket who knew Mathew.

We again thanked Captain Morris and Sandy. And after they departed, I put my arm around Shirley and said, "Well, honey whatcha know, dad was a time traveler too. Wish I had known that when I visited his grave at Cerlot, France in 1969 and again during my 1944 timeline."

* * * * *

Now, as time continues its relentless passage, Shirley and I sit at our kitchen table, savoring a glass of wine, and listening to music on our CD player. Sometimes we play German music which brings back a million memories, of not only our vacations to Germany, but also of my trips back in time. Perhaps it is a function of the aging process, but I know Shirley is tired of my gerrymandering around in time. For that matter, Bob also has all but told me to cool it.

Thus, on this night as we sit, sip, and remember, a very difficult decision for me emerged.... ***That's all folks!...*** *I thank each and every one of you so dearly for reading the journals of my escapades in time. I had lots of fun, and hope you did too.*

And now, finally, I say so long, and like General George Smith Patton so proudly professed, "Perhaps I'll live again to fight other battles on another day... Yes, perhaps...life does spring eternal doesn't it?, and as time trudges on, who knows?"

* * * * *

Therefore I, *Frederick Dale Mitchell*, respectfully consign the following to the aegis of time:

* * * * *

Fred D. Mitchell as:

When Rivers Meet

Colonel, 2nd Illinois Cavalry

Captain, C-Troop, 6th US. Cavalry

The Hindenburg's Farewell

Reporter, Aboard the Hindenburg

December 7th , 1941

Commander, US. Navy, At Pearl Harbor

Beyond The Arc

Citizen, Highlands of Ole Scotland

Western Front 1918 and 1944

Lieutenant/Capitan, US Army, Battle of the Bulge

BIBLIOGRAPHY

Brownlow, Donald Grey, *Panzer Baron,* The Christopher Publishing House, North Quincy Massachusetts, 02171, 1975

Eisenhower, John S. D, *The Bitter Woods,* G. P. Putnam & Son, New York, 1969

Gott, J. Richard, *Time Travel in Einstein's Universe*, Houghton Mifflin Company, Boston New York, 2001

Hamilton, John, *Aircraft of World War I, ABDO* Publishing Company, Edina Minnesota, 55435, 2004

Merriam, Robert E., *Dark December,* Ziff-Davis Publishing Company, Chicago and New York, 1947

Toland, John, *The Last 100 Days,* Random House, New York, 1966

Wikipedia on-line Encyclopedia; General George Smith Patton, Jr. and General Hasso Eccard von Manteuffel

ILLUSTRATION CREDITS.

The War; Geoffrey C. Ward and Ken Burns, Alfred A Knopf, New York, 2007

1. Soldier with bazooka, Front matter, page iii; National Archives and Records Administration
2. Soldier in foxhole, page328; National Archives & Records Administration.
3. Tanks in woods, page 295; National Archives & Records Administration.

...Manteuffel photos...Panzer Baron, Donald Grey Brownlow, Christopher Publishing House, North Quincy Massachusetts, 02171, 1975

...General and Frau Manteuffel, Diessen Ammersee, May 1974, Author's collection.

...Correspondence with von Manteuffel: Author's collection